THE TWO TARZANS

Tarzan tossed his weapons to the ground. "Throw down your bow and spear," he said.

The other looked puzzled. "Why?" he asked.

"Because I am going to kill you, but I will give you your chance."

The other threw down his weapons. "I don't know why you want to kill me," he said, "but you are at liberty to try." He showed no fear.

"I am going to kill you because you stole my name, and stole the women and children of my friends—and this woman with you. My friends think it was I; and they have turned against me. Now I kill!"

Suddenly Sandra stepped between the two men, facing Tarzan. "You must listen to me," she said. "*You must not kill this man!*"

By Edgar Rice Burroughs
Published by Ballantine Books:

TARZAN
and the Madman

Edgar Rice Burroughs

BALLANTINE BOOKS • NEW YORK

ISBN 0-345-35037-5

This authorized edition published by arrangement
with Edgar Rice Burroughs, Inc.

Printed in Canada

First U.S. Printing: February 1965
Tenth U.S. Printing: May 1987

First Canadian Printing: April 1965

Cover illustration by Boris Vallejo

TABLE OF CONTENTS

ONE . . Friends or Enemies

MAN HAS FIVE SENSES, some of which are more or less well developed, some more or less atrophied. The beasts have these same senses, and always one and sometimes two of them are developed to a point beyond the conception of civilized man. These two are the sense of smell and the sense of hearing. The eyesight of birds is phenomenal, but that of many beasts is poor. Your dog invariably verifies the testimony of his eyes by coming close and smelling of you. He knows that his eyes might deceive him, but his nose never.

And the beasts appear to have another sense, unknown to man. No one knows what it is, but many of us have seen demonstrations of it at one time or another during our lives—a dog suddenly bristling and growling at night and glaring intently and half-fearfully at something you cannot see. There are those who maintain that dogs can see disembodied spirits, or at least sense their presence.

Tarzan of the Apes had the five senses that men and beasts share in common, and he had them all developed far beyond those of an ordinary man. In addition, he possessed that strange other sense of which I have spoken. It was nothing he could have defined. It is even possible he was not aware that he possessed it.

But now as he moved cautiously along a jungle trail, he felt a presentiment that he was being stalked—the hunter was being hunted. None of his objective senses verified the conclusion, but the ape-man could not shake off the conviction.

So now he moved even more warily, for the instinct of the wild beast for caution warned him not to ignore the portent. It was not fear that prompted him, for he did not know fear as you and I. He had no fear of death, who had faced it so often. He was merely activated more or less unconsciously by Nature's first law—self-preservation. Like the dog that senses the presence of a ghost at night, he felt that whatever had impinged upon his consciousness was malign rather than beneficent.

Tarzan had many enemies. There were his natural enemies, such as Numa the lion and Sheeta the panther. These he had had always, ever since the day he had been born in the lonely cabin on the far West Coast. He had learned of them even as he suckled at the hairy breast of his foster-mother—Kala the great she-ape. He had learned to avoid them, but never to fear them; and he had learned how to bait and annoy them.

But his worst enemies were men—men whom he had to punish for their transgressions—African natives and white men, to him, Gomangani and Tarmangani in the language of his fierce, shaggy people.

Numa and Sheeta he admired—his world would have been desolate without them; but the men who were his enemies he held only in contempt. He did not hate them. Hate was for them to feel in their small, warped brains. It was not for the Lord of the Jungle.

Nothing out of the ordinary may go unchallenged or uninvestigated by the wild beast which would survive; and so Tarzan took to the trees and doubled back upon his trail, directed by a natural assumption that if he were being stalked the stalker had been following behind him.

As he swung down wind through the trees, following the middle terrace where the lower branches would better conceal him from the eyes of the enemy on the ground, he realized that the direction of the wind would carry the scent spoor of him he sought away from him and that he must depend wholly upon his ears for the first information of the presence of a foe. He commenced to feel a little foolish as the ordinary noises of the jungle were unbroken by any that might suggest a menace to him. He commenced to compare himself with Wappi the antelope, which is suspicious and fearful of everything. And at last he was upon the point of turning back when his keen ears detected a sound that was not of the primitive jungle. It was the clink of metal upon metal, and it came faintly from afar.

Now there was a point to his progress and a destination, and he moved more swiftly but none the less silently in the direction from which the sound had come. The sound that he had heard connoted men, for the wild denizens of the jungle do not clink metal against metal. Presently he heard other sounds, the muffled tramp of booted feet, a cough, and then, very faintly, voices.

Now he swung to the left and made a wide detour that he might circle his quarry and come upon it from behind and upwind, that thus he might determine its strength and composition before risking being seen himself. He skirted a clearing which lay beside a river and presently reached a position to which Usha the wind bore the scent spoor of a party of blacks and whites. Tarzan judged there to be some twenty or thirty men, with not more than two or three whites among them.

When he came within sight of them, they had already reached the clearing beside the river and were preparing to make camp. There were two white men and a score or more of blacks. It might have been a harmless hunting party, but Tarzan's premonition kept him aloof. Concealed by the foliage of a tree, he watched. Later, when it was dark, he would come closer and listen, for he might not wholly ignore the warning his strange sense had given him.

Presently another noise came to his ears, came from up the river—the splash of paddles in the water. Tarzan settled down to wait. Perhaps friendly natives were coming, perhaps hostile; for there were still savage tribes in this part of the forest.

The men below him gave no signs that they were aware of the approach of the canoes, the noise of which was all too plain to the ape-man. Even when four canoes came into sight on the river, the men in the camp failed to discover them. Tarzan wondered how such stupid creatures managed to survive. He never expected anything better from white men, but he felt that the natives should long since have been aware of the approach of the strangers.

Tarzan saw that there were two white men in the leading canoe, and even at a distance he sensed something familiar in one of them. Now one of the blacks in the camp discovered the newcomers and shouted a warning to attract his fellows. At the same time the occupants of the leading canoe saw the party on the shore and, changing their direction, led the others towards the camp. The two white men, accompanied by some askaris, went down to meet them; and presently, after a conversation which Tarzan could not overhear, the four canoes were dragged up on the bank and the newcomers prepared to make camp beside the other party.

TWO . . The Two Safaris

As THE TWO WHITE MEN stepped from their canoe, Pelham Dutton was not greatly impressed by their appearance. They were hard and sinister looking, but he greeted them cordially.

Bill Gantry, Dutton's guide and hunter, stepped forward toward one of the men with outstretched hand. "Hello, Tom, Long time no see;" then he turned toward Dutton. "This is Tom Crump, Mr. Dutton, an old timer around here."

Crump nodded crustily. "This here's Minsky," he said, indicating his companion.

From a tree at the edge of the clearing, Tarzan recognized Crump as a notorious ivory poacher whom he had run out of the country a couple of years before. He knew him for an all around rotter and a dangerous man, wanted by the authorities of at least two countries. The other three men, Dutton, Gantry and Minsky, he had never seen before. Dutton made a good impression upon the ape-man. Gantry made no impression at all; but he mentally catalogued Ivan Minsky as the same type as Crump.

Crump and Minsky were occupied for a while, directing the unloading of the canoes and the setting up of their camp. Dutton had walked back to his own camp, but Gantry remained with the newcomers.

When Crump was free he turned to Gantry. "What you doin' here, Bill?" he asked; then he nodded toward Dutton, who was standing outside his tent. "Who's that guy, the law?" It was evident that he was nervous and suspicious.

"You don't have to worry none about him," said Gantry, reassuringly. "He ain't even a Britisher. He's an American."

"Hunting?" asked Crump.

"We was," replied Gantry. "I was guide and hunter for this Dutton and a rich old bloke named Timothy Pickerall—you know, Pickerall's Ale. Comes from Edinburgh, I think. Well, the old bloke has his daughter, Sandra, with him. Well, one day, a great big guy comes into camp wearing nothing but a G string. He's a big guy and not bad-lookin'. He said his name was Tarzan of the Apes. Ever hear of him?"

Crump grimaced. "I sure have," he said. "He's a bad 'un. He run me out of good elephant country two years ago."

"Well, it seems that the Pickerall gal and her old man had heard of this here Tarzan. They said he was some sort of a Lord or Duke or something, and they treated him like a long-lost brother. So one day they goes hunting, and the girl goes out alone with this here Tarzan, and they never come back; so we thought they got killed or something, and we hunt for them for about a week until we meets up with a native what had seen them. He said this here Tarzan had the girl's hands tied behind her and was leading her along with a rope around her neck; so then we knew she'd been abducted. So old man Pickerall gets a heart attack and nearly croaks, and this here Dutton says he'll find her if it's the last thing he does on earth, because the guy's soft on this Pickerall gal. So the old man says he'll give a £1000 reward for the safe return of his daughter, and £500 for Tarzan dead or alive. The old man wanted to come along, but on account of his heart he didn't dare. So that's why we're here; and you don't have to worry none about nothin'."

"So you'd like to find this here Tarzan, would you?" demanded Crump.

"I sure would."

"Well, so would I. I got somethin' to settle with him, and with £500 on his head it's gonna be worth my while to give a little time to this here matter; and I'm the guy that can find him."

"How's that?" demanded Gantry.

"Well, I just been up in the wild Waruturi country, aimin' to do a little tradin'. They're a bad lot, those Waruturi— cannibals and all that, but I gets along swell with old Mutimbwa, their chief. I done him a good turn once, and I always take him a lot of presents. And while I was there, they told me about a naked white man who had stolen a lot of their women and children. They say he lives up beyond the great thorn forest that grows along the foothills of the Ruturi Mountains. That's bad country in there. I don't guess no white man's ever been in it; but the natives give it a bad name.

"Some of the Waruturi followed this guy once, and they know pretty much where he holes up; but when they got beyond the thorn forest, they got scared and turned back, for all that country in there is taboo." Crump was silent for a moment; then he said, "Yes, I guess I'll join up with you fellows and help find the girl and that Tarzan guy."

"You'd like a shot at your old friend Tarzan, wouldn't you?" said Gantry.

"And at the £1500," added Crump.

"Nothin' doin'," said Gantry. "That's mine."

Crump grinned. "Same old Gantry, ain't you?" he demanded "But this time I got you over a barrel. I can go in alone, for I know the way; and if you try to follow, you'll end up in the Waruturi cooking pots. All I got to do is tell 'em you're comin' and they'll be waitin' for you with poisoned bamboo splinters in every trail. The only reason I'd take you along at all is because the more guns we have, the better the chance we got."

"O.K.," said Gantry. "You win. I was only kiddin' anyhow."

"Does Dutton get a cut?" asked Crump.

"No, he's doin' it because he's soft on the girl. Anyway, he's got skads of boodle."

"We'll have to cut Minsky in."

"The hell we will!" exclaimed Gantry.

"Now wait a second, Bill," said Crump. "Me and him split everything fifty-fifty. He's a good guy to have for a friend, too; but look out for him if he don't like you. He's got an awful nervous trigger finger. You'd better see that he likes you."

"You're the same old chiseler, aren't you?" said Gantry, disgustedly.

"I'd rather have a chisel used on me than a gun," replied Crump, meaningly.

The brief equatorial twilight had passed on and darkness had fallen upon the camp as the white men finished their evening meal. The black boys squatted around their small cooking fires while a larger beast fire was being prepared to discourage the approach of the great cats. The nocturnal noises of the forest lent a mystery to the jungle that Pelham Dutton sensed keenly. To the other whites, long accustomed to it, and to the natives to whom it was a lifelong experience, this distance-muted diapason of the wilderness brought no reaction—the crash of a falling tree in the distance, the crickets, the shrill piping call of the cicadae, the perpetual chorus of the frogs, and the doleful cry of the lemur to his mate, and, far away, the roar of a lion.

Dutton shuddered—he was thinking that out there somewhere in that hideous world of darkness and savagery and mystery was the girl he loved in the clutches of a fiend. He wished that she knew that he loved her. He had never told her, and he knew now that he had not realized it himself until she had been taken from him.

During the evening meal, Crump had told him what he had heard in the Waruturi country, and that no woman that the ape-man, as Crump called him, had stolen had ever been returned. Dutton's waning hope had been slightly renewed by Crump's assurance that he could lead them to the haunts of the abductor, and Dutton tried to console himself with the thought that if he could not effect a rescue he might at least have vengeance.

The beast fire had been lighted, and now the flames were leaping high illuminating the entire camp. Suddenly a black cried out in astonishment and alarm, and as the whites looked up they saw a bronzed giant, naked but for a G string, slowly approaching.

Crump leaped to his feet. "It's the damned ape-man himself," he cried; and, drawing his pistol, fired point-blank at Tarzan.

THREE . . Hunted

CRUMP'S SHOT WENT WILD AND, so instantaneous are the reactions of Tarzan, it seemed that almost simultaneously an arrow drove through Crump's right shoulder, and his pistol arm was useless.

The incident had occurred so suddenly and ended so quickly that momentarily the entire camp was in confusion; and in that moment, Tarzan melted into the blackness of the forest.

"You fool!" cried Dutton to Crump. "He was coming into camp. We might have questioned him." And then he raised his voice and cried, "Tarzan, Tarzan, come back. I give you my word that you will not be harmed. Where is Miss Pickerall? Come back and tell us."

Tarzan heard the question, but it was meaningless to him; and he did not return. He had no desire to be shot at again by Crump, whom he believed had fired at him for purely personal reasons of revenge.

That night he lay up in a tree wondering before he fell asleep who Miss Pickerall might be and why anyone should think that he knew her whereabouts.

Early the next morning he stalked a small buck and made a kill. Squatting beside it, he filled his belly while Dango the hyena and Ungo the jackal circled him enviously, waiting for his leavings.

Later in the day he became aware that there were a number of natives ahead of him, but this was still a friendly country in which there were no natives hostile to the ape-man. He had ranged it for years and knew that the natives looked upon him as a friend and protector; and so he was less cautious than usual, having no thought of danger until a spear flashed past him from ambush so close that he felt the wind of its passing.

If you would kill or cripple a wild beast it is well to see that your first missile does not miss him. Almost before

14

his assailant could determine whether or not his cast had been true, Tarzan had swung into the lower terraces of the forest and disappeared.

Making a wide detour, Tarzan circled about and came back, cautiously, along the middle terrace, to learn the identity of his assailant; and presently he came upon some twenty warriors huddled together and evidently suffering from an excess of terror.

"You missed him," one of them was saying, "and he will come and take vengeance upon us."

"We were fools," said another. "We should have waited until he came to our village. There we would have treated him like a friend; and then, when he was off his guard, fallen upon him and bound him."

"I do not like any of it," said a third. "I am afraid of Tarzan of the Apes."

"But the reward was very large," insisted another. "They say that it is so great that it would buy a hundred wives for every man in the village, and cows and goats and chickens the number of which has never been seen."

This was all very puzzling to the ape man, and he determined to solve the mystery before he went farther.

He knew where lay the village of these black men, and after dark he approached it and lay up in a tree nearby. Tarzan knew the habits of these people, and he knew that because it was a quiet evening without dancing or drinking they would soon all be wrapped in slumber on their sleeping mats within their huts and that only a single sentry would be on guard before the king's hut; so he waited with the infinite patience of the beast watching the lair of its quarry, and when utter quiet had fallen upon the village he approached the palisade from the rear. He ran the last few steps and, like a cat, scrambled to the top; then he dropped quietly into the shadows beyond.

Swiftly and with every sense alert he planned his retreat. He noted a large tree, one branch of which overhung the palisade. This would answer his purpose, though he would have to pass several huts to reach it. The guard before the chief's hut had built a little fire to keep him warm, for the night was chill; but it was burning low—an indication to Tarzan that the man might be dozing.

Keeping in the denser shadows of the huts, the ape-man moved silently toward his quarry. He could hear the heavy breathing of the sleepers within the huts, and he had no fear of detection by them; but there was always the danger that some yapping cur might discover him.

The light of the stars moving across the face of a planet makes no noise. As noiseless was the progress of the ape-man; and so he came to the chief's hut, undiscovered, and there he found what he had expected—a dozing sentry. Tarzan crept up behind the man. Simultaneously, steel-thewed fingers seized the man's throat and a strong hand was clapped over his mouth. A voice spoke in his ear: "Silence, and I will not kill."

The man struggled as Tarzan threw him across his shoulder. For a moment the fellow was paralyzed with terror, but presently he jerked his mouth momentarily from Tarzan's palm and voiced a terrified scream; then the ape-man closed upon the fellow's windpipe and commenced to run toward the tree that overhung the palisade; but already the village was aroused. Curs came yapping from the huts, followed by warriors sleepy-eyed and confused. A huge warrior buck blocked his way; but the Lord of the Jungle threw himself against him before the fellow could use his weapon, hurling him to the ground, and then, leaping over him, ran for the tree with curs and warriors now in hot pursuit.

Wind-driven as a sapling, the tree leaned toward the palisade at an angle of some forty-five degrees; and before the foremost warrior could overtake him, Tarzan, running up the inclined bole, had disappeared in the foliage. A moment later he dropped to the ground outside the palisade, quite confident that the natives would not pursue him there, at least not until they had wasted much time and talk, which is a characteristic of the African savage, and by that time he would be far away in the forest with his captive. Now he loosened his grip on the black's throat and set him on his feet. "Come with me quietly," he said, "and you will not be harmed."

The black trembled. "Who are you?" he asked. It was too dark for him to see his captor's features, and previously he had been in no position to see them.

"I am Tarzan," replied the ape-man.

Now the black trembled violently. "Do not harm me, Bwana Tarzan," he begged, "and I will do anything that you wish."

Tarzan did not reply, but led the man on into the forest in silence.

He stopped just beyond the edge of the clearing and took his captive into a tree from which point of vantage he could see if any pursuit developed.

"Now," he said, when he had settled himself comfortably upon a limb, "I shall ask you some questions. When you answer, speak true words if you would live."

"Yes, Bwana Tarzan," replied the black, "I will speak only true words."

"Why did the warriors of your village attack me today and try to kill me?"

"The drums told us to kill you because you were coming to steal our women and our children."

"Your people have known Tarzan for a long time," said the ape-man. "They know that he does not steal women or children."

"But they say that Tarzan's heart has gone bad and that now he does steal women and children. The Waruturi have seen him taking women to his village, which lies beyond the thorn forest that grows along the little hills at the foot of the Ruturi Mountains."

"You take the word of the Waruturi?" demanded Tarzan. "They are bad people. They are cannibals and liars, as all men know."

"Yes, Bwana, all men know that the Waruturi are cannibals and liars; but three men of my own village saw you, Bwana, less than a moon ago when you went through our country leading a white girl with a rope about her neck."

"You are not speaking true words, now," said Tarzan. "I have not been in your country for many moons."

"I am not saying that I saw you, Bwana," replied the black. "I am only repeating what the three men said they saw."

"Go back to your village," said the ape-man, "and tell your people that it was not Tarzan whom the three warriors saw, but some man with a bad heart whom Tarzan is going to find and kill so that your women and children need fear no longer."

Now Tarzan had a definite goal, and the following morning he set out in the direction of the Ruturi Mountains, still mystified by the origin of these reports of his atrocities but determined to solve the enigma and bring the guilty one to justice.

Shortly after noon, Tarzan caught the scent spoor of a native approaching him along the trail. He knew that there was only one man, and so he made no effort to conceal himself. Presently he came face to face with a sleek, ebony warrior. The fellow's eyes dilated in consternation as he recognized the ape-man, and simultaneously he hurled his spear at Tarzan and turned and ran as fast as his legs would carry him.

Tarzan had recognized the black as the son of a friendly chief; and the incident, coupled with the recent experiences, seemed to indicate that every man's hand was against him, even those of his friends.

He was quite certain now that someone was impersonating him; and, as he must find this man, he might not overlook a single clue; therefore he pursued the warrior and presently dropped upon his shoulders from the foliage above the trail.

The warrior struggled, but quite hopelessly, in the grip of the ape-man. "Why would you have killed me?" demanded Tarzan. "I, who have been your friend!"

"The drums," said the warrior; and then he told much the same story that the black sentry had told Tarzan the previous night.

"And what else did the drums tell you?" demanded the ape-man.

"They told us that four white men with a great safari are searching for you and the white girl that you stole."

So that was why Crump had shot at him. It explained also the other man's question: "Where is Miss Pickerall?"

"Tell your people," said Tarzan to the black warrior, "that it was not Tarzan who stole their women and children, that it was not Tarzan who stole the white girl. It is someone with a bad heart who has stolen Tarzan's name."

"A demon, perhaps," suggested the warrior.

"Man or demon, Tarzan will find him," said the ape-man. "If the whites come this way, tell them what I have said."

FOUR .. Captured

THE GLOOM OF THE FOREST lay heavy upon Sandra Pickerall, blinding her to the beauties of the orchids, the delicate tracery of the ferns, the graceful loops of the giant lianas festooned from tree to tree. She was aware only that it was sinister, mysterious, horrible.

At first she had been afraid of the man leading her like a dumb beast to slaughter with a rope about her neck; but as the days passed and he had offered her no harm her fear of him lessened. He was an enigma to her. For all the weary days that they had tramped through the interminable forest, he had scarcely spoken a word. Upon his countenance she often noticed an expression of puzzlement and doubt. He was a large, well built man, possibly in his late twenties, she thought, with a rather nice, open face. He did not look at all like a scoundrel or a villain, she concluded; but what did he want of her? Where was he taking her? Now as they sat down to rest and to eat, she demanded for the hundredth time, "Who are you? Where are you taking me? Why don't you answer me?"

The man shook his head as though trying to shake the cobwebs from his mind. He looked at her intently.

"Who am I? Why, I am Tarzan. I know I am Tarzan; but they call me God—but,"—he leaned closer toward her— "sh-h-h, I am not God; but don't tell them that I told you."

"Who are 'they'?" she demanded.

"The Alemtejos," he replied. "Da Gama says that I am God, but old Ruiz says that I am a devil who has been sent to bring bad luck to the Alemtejos."

"Who are da Gama and Ruiz?" asked the girl, wondering at this sudden break in the man's silence and hoping to stimulate it by her questions.

"Da Gama is king," replied the man, "and Ruiz is high priest. He wants to get rid of me because he doesn't want a god around. You see, a god is more powerful than a high priest. At first he tried to get da Gama to kill me; but da Gama wouldn't do that; so finally Ruiz said that a god was no good without a goddess. Well, after a while, da Gama agreed to that and told me to go and find a goddess; otherwise I should be killed. You are the goddess. I am taking you back, and now they won't kill me."

"Why do you go back?" she demanded. "This high priest will only find some other excuse to kill you."

"Where would I go, if I didn't go back to Alemtejo?" he demanded.

"Go back to where you came from," said the girl.

Again that puzzled expression crossed his face. "I can't do that," he said. "I came from heaven. Da Gama said so; and I don't know how to get back. He said I floated down from heaven. In fact, they all say so. They say that they saw me; but I do not know how to float up again, and if I did I would not know where to find heaven. However, I do not think that I am God at all. I am Tarzan."

"I tell you what you do," said Sandra. "You come back with me to my people. They will be kind, if you bring me back. I will see that they do not harm you."

He shook his head. "No, I must do as da Gama says, or he will be very angry."

She tried to argue the question with him, but he was adamant. The girl came to the conclusion that the man must be simple-minded, and that, having been given an idea by da Gama, it had become fixed in his mind to such an extent that he was unable to act on any other suggestion; yet he did not look a half-wit. He had a well shaped head and an intelligent face. His speech was that of an educated man, his attitude toward her that of a gentleman.

Sandra had heard stories of Tarzan of the Apes, but all that she had heard had convinced her that he was far too intelligent to permit him even to entertain the idea that he might be a god, and as for running at the beck and call of this da Gama or anyone else she was quite sure that would be out of the question; yet this man insisted that he was Tarzan. With a shrug, Sandra gave up in despair.

As they took up their journey again after their rest, the man continued talking. It was as though there had been a dam across his reservoir of speech, and now that it was broken he felt relieved that the words would flow.

"You are very beautiful," he said, suddenly. "You will

make a beautiful goddess. I am sure that da Gama will be pleased. It took me a long time to find you. I brought them black women and children, but they did not want these for goddesses; so many of them were fed to the guardians of Alemtejo. One has to offer sacrifices to them occasionally, even a god; so now I always try to take a woman or a child in with me. The guardians of Alemtejo do not care so much for the flesh of men."

"Who are the guardians of Alemtejo, who eat human beings?" demanded Sandra; but her question was not answered, for at the instant that she voiced it a score of painted warriors rose up about them.

"The Waruturi," whispered the false Tarzan.

"It is Tarzan," cried Mutimbwa the chief.

Two warriors leaped forward with levelled spears, but Mutimbwa the chief stepped between them and the white man. "Do not kill him," he said. "We will take them to the village and summon the tribe to a feast."

"But he stole our women and children," objected one of the warriors.

"So much the better, then, that he die slowly; so that he will remember," said Mutimbwa.

"You understand what they are saying?" Sandra asked the man.

He nodded. "Yes, do you?"

"Enough," she said.

"Do not worry," said the man. "I shall escape; and then I shall come and get you."

"How can you escape?" she demanded.

"I can try," he said; "and if I am God, as da Gama has said I am, it should be easy for me to escape; and if I am Tarzan, as I know I am, it should be very easy."

They were moving along the forest trail now with blacks in front of them and behind them. It did not seem to Sandra that it would be an easy thing for even a god to escape. Suddenly he who said that he was Tarzan raised his head and voiced a piercing scream, strange and weird. A black struck him with the haft of his spear, and told him to be quiet; but that cry had made the Waruturi nervous, and they kept casting apprehensive glances about them.

From far away came an answering cry. The blacks jabbered excitedly among themselves, and often Sandra caught the word for demon. Mutimbwa the chief urged the party into a trot.

Apparently the entire company was seized with nervous apprehension.

"Something answered your cry," said the girl to the man. "What was it?"

He smiled at her. "One of God's servants," he said. "Presently they will come and take me away."

The girl was mystified. The thing was uncanny, for the sound that had come to them could not have come from a human throat.

Presently they came to a more open part of the forest and, to Sandra's relief, the gait was reduced to a walk. She had eaten neither regularly nor much since her capture, and the long and exhausting marches had sapped her strength. Suddenly she was startled by a loud cry of alarm from behind her and, turning, she saw what was to her as fearsome a sight as it must have been to the genuinely terrified blacks— a band of huge, man-like apes, snarling and growling, had charged among the Waruturi. Their mighty fangs, their huge muscular arms and hands were wreaking havoc with the terrified blacks. With one accord, they bolted, carrying Sandra Pickerall along with them. The great apes pursued them for a short distance and then turned back. When Mutimbwa had succeeded in quieting and rallying his warriors, it was discovered that the white prisoner, whom they thought was Tarzan, had disappeared.

So God had escaped! Sandra was more than half-glad that she had not escaped with him, for those great, hairy apes seemed even more terrifying than the blacks. The blacks were men. She might persuade them, in view of the ransom that she knew she could offer, to take her back to her people; but then Sandra did not know the Waruturi or their customs. There was, however, just one little doubt in her mind. She had noticed, from the first moment that she had been able to note these warriors carefully, that there was not one of them but wore golden ornaments. Armlets, anklets, of solid gold, were common; and nearly all of them wore golden rings in their ears. What temptation would her father's money be to a people possessing so much wealth as these?

When they reached the palisaded village of the Waruturi chief, she saw even greater evidence of gold and wealth.

Once inside the village, she was turned over to the women who struck her and spit upon her and tore most of her clothes from her. They would have killed her had not Mutimbwa the chief intervened.

"You have done enough," said the chief. "Leave her alone; and the night after this night we shall feast."

"You are the chief?" asked Sandra.

Mutimbwa nodded. "I am Mutimbwa the chief," he said.

"Take me back to my people," said the girl, "and you can name your own ransom." She spoke in broken Swahili.

Mutimbwa laughed at her. "If the white man has anything we want, we will go and take it away from him," he said.

"What are you going to do with me?" demanded Sandra. Mutimbwa pointed at a cooking pot and rubbed his belly.

FIVE . . Cannibal Feast

THE APE-MAN WAS IN NEW and unfamiliar country now, as he approached the illy-defined borders of the Waruturis' domain. He knew these people by reputation only. He knew that they were fierce, uncivilized savages and cannibals; but his only concern as far as they were concerned was to be constantly on guard against them.

His business was to trail the white man who was impersonating him, and destroy him. The rescue of the white girl was incidental. If he could find her and take her back to her people, well and good; but first he must destroy the impostor who was stealing the women and children of those who had been his friends.

The second night since he had entered the Waruturi country had fallen. He had seen no Waruturi nor had he come upon the trail of the impostor and the girl. His immediate plan was to enter the Ruturi Mountains and search there.

Late in the afternoon he had made a kill and had eaten. Now he was lying up for the night in the fork of a great tree. The night sounds of the jungle were lulling him to sleep when there came faintly to his ears above these the sound of drums. The ape-man listened intently. The drums were calling the tribe to a feast that would be held the following night. He guessed that they were Waruturi drums.

He put together the things that he knew. The white girl and her captor would have had to pass through the Waruturi country. The Waruturi were cannibals. They were summoning their people from other villages to a feast. It was unlikely that this would be true unless it were to be a cannibal feast. Tarzan decided to investigate. The direction from which the sounds came and their volume gave him some idea of the location of the village and its distance. He settled himself comfortably in the crotch of the tree, and slept. Tomorrow he would go to the village.

The second night of Sandra Pickerall's captivity was approaching. The village of Mutimbwa the chief was crowded. All day, warriors and women and children had been straggling in from other villages. Sandra could see them through the doorway of the hut where she was imprisoned. As she estimated their number, she was grimly aware that there would not be enough of her to go around. Even in the face of so horrible an end, the girl smiled. That was the stuff of which she was made.

At last they came for her. The cooking pots were simmering. Five bleating goats were trussed up and lying beneath the great tree in front of the chief's hut. Sandra was dragged to a place beside the goats. The witch-doctor and a few bucks commenced to dance around them. They were chanting, and the drums were keeping melancholy time.

Suddenly, with a loud scream, the witch-doctor darted in and fell upon a goat, severing its jugular with his knife; then the chanting rose to a wail, and all the villagers joined in.

Sandra sensed that this was in the nature of a religious rite. She saw that it was a priest who cut up the body of the goat. He mumbled gibberish over each piece as he handed it to a warrior, who in turn took it to a woman who transferred it to one of the cooking pots.

One by one the goats were slaughtered and butchered thus. The witch-doctor was dismembering the fifth goat. Sandra knew that it would be her turn next. She tried to be brave. She must not show fear before these bestial savages. The goats had bleated, but not she. She thought of her father and her friends. She thought of Pelham Dutton. She prayed that in searching for her they might not fall into the hands of the Waruturi.

The last morsel of the fifth goat had been disposed of in a cooking pot. The witch-doctor was coming toward her. The warriors were dancing about her. The chant rose in volume and savagery.

The final moment had come. The witch-doctor darted toward her, blood-smeared hands grasping his bloody knife, the knife which was to sever her jugular. Suddenly the witch-doctor stopped, voiced a single scream of agony and collapsed upon the ground, the haft of an arrow protruding from his heart. Simultaneously, a white man, naked but for a G-string, dropped from the tree above to the ground beside her. Into the very midst of the dancing cannibals he dropped just as the dancing ceased and every eye was upon the body of the witch-doctor.

It was all done so quickly that afterward no one, probably, could have told how it was accomplished. One moment the victim was there and the witch-doctor's knife was almost at her jugular. The next instant the witch-doctor was dead and the captive was gone.

Even Sandra could not have told how it was done. She had stood there waiting for imminent death when suddenly she was seized about the waist and lifted from the ground. The next instant she was in the tree above the chief's hut and was being borne away through the foliage in the darkness of the night. How they surmounted the palisade, she never knew. She was half unconscious from surprise and fright as they crossed the clearing. The first thing that she could ever recall was sitting high in the branches of a tree in the forest with a man's strong arm about her to keep her from falling.

"Who are you?" she gasped.

"I am Tarzan of the Apes," replied a deep voice.

"Da Gama must have been right," she said. "You must be God, for nobody else could have rescued me." The voice had seemed different, but this could not be other than her strange captor who had promised to come and rescue her.

"I don't know what you are talking about," said Tarzan.

"Only what you told me yesterday," she said, "that you thought you were Tarzan but da Gama insisted you were God."

"I did not see you yesterday," said the ape-man. "I have never seen you before. I am Tarzan of the Apes."

"You mean to tell me that you did not steal me from my father's camp and bring me here to this country?"

"That was another man who is impersonating me. I am searching for him to kill him. Do you know where he is? Was he also a captive of the Waruturi?"

"No, he escaped; but he promised to come back and rescue me."

"Tell me something about him," said the ape-man.

"He was a strange creature," replied the girl. "I think he had been a gentleman. He did not harm me, and he was always considerate and respectful."

"Why did he steal you, then?"

"He said that da Gama insisted that he was a god, and had sent him out to find a white woman to be his goddess. I think"

—she hesitated—"I think he was not quite right in the head; but he was so certain that he was Tarzan of the Apes. Are you sure that you are?"

"Quite," said the ape-man.

"Why did you rescue me?" she asked. "How did you know that I was in the village of the Waruturi?"

"I did not know. The drums told me that the Waruturi were feasting tonight; and knowing them to be cannibals and knowing that you were in this part of the forest, I came to their village to investigate."

"And now you will take me back to my father?"

"Yes," said the ape-man.

"You know where his safari is?"

"There is a safari with four white men looking for me to kill me," said Tarzan with a grim smile. "That is doubtless the safari of your father."

"There were only three white men with our safari," said Sandra, "my father, Pelham Dutton, and our guide and hunter, a man by the name of Gantry."

"There was a man by the name of Crump with this safari. He shot at me but missed."

"There was no man by the name of Crump with our safari."

"What did your father look like?"

After the girl had described her father to him, Tarzan shook his head. "Your father is not with that safari." But when she described Dutton and Gantry he recognized them.

"Crump and the fourth man joined Dutton and Gantry some time ago. Crump is a bad man. I don't know the other one; but if he is ranging with Crump he is no good either," Tarzan told her.

Sandra Pickerall slept that night on a rude platform that Tarzan built for her high among the branches of a patriarch of the jungle, and she slept well for she was exhausted; and she slept without fear for there was something about the man with her which imbued her with confidence.

When she awoke in the morning she was alone, and when she realized her situation she was afraid. She was totally unprepared to cope with the dangers of the forest, nor had she the remotest idea in which direction to search for the safari that was looking for her.

She wondered why the man had deserted her. It seemed so inconsistent with the thing he had done the night before in risking his life to save her from the Waruturi. She came to the conclusion that all the wild men of the jungle were irresponsible and, perhaps, a little bit insane. It didn't seem credible that a white man in his right senses would run around almost naked in the jungle in preference to living in a civilized environment.

She was very hungry, but she hadn't the remotest idea how to obtain food. Some of the fruits of the forest trees she knew to be safe; but she saw none around her which she recognized, and she did not dare eat the others. It all seemed very hopeless, so hopeless that she commenced to wonder how long it would take before she died of starvation, if some beast of the jungle did not kill her in the meantime.

And then at the very depths of despondency, she heard a noise in the tree behind her and, turning, saw her rescuer of the night before swing lightly to the branch at her side, one arm laden with fruits.

"You are hungry?" he asked.

"Very."

"Then eat; and when you have eaten, we will start out in search of the safari of your friends."

"I thought you had deserted me," she said.

"I will not leave you" he replied, "until I have returned you safely to your people."

Tarzan could only guess at the general direction in which to hunt for the safari of the girl's friends; but he knew that eventually he could find it, though the great forests of Central Africa cover over three hundred thousand square miles of territory.

* * *

The men of Dutton's safari were hungry for fresh meat; and so the white men decided to remain in camp for a day and do some hunting. Early in the morning they set out, each in a different direction, with their gun-bearers. At perhaps a mile from camp, Crump stumbled upon a water hole evidently much used by the jungle beasts; and finding concealment among some bushes, he lay down to wait for his quarry to come to him.

He had been lying in concealment for about an hour without seeing any signs of game when he heard someone approaching. He could hear their voices before he saw them and thought that he recognized one as being that of a woman; so he was not surprised when Tarzan and Sandra Pickerall came into view.

Crump's lips curled in a nasty grin as he cautiously raised his rifle and took careful aim at the ape-man. When he squeezed the trigger, Tarzan pitched forward upon his face, blood gushing from a head wound.

SIX . . In Cold Blood

As TARZAN FELL, Crump leaped to his feet and called the girl by name as he strode toward her.

"Who are you?" she demanded.

"I am one of the guys that's looking for you," he said. "My name is Tom Crump."

"Why did you shoot him?" she demanded. "You've killed him."

"I hope so," said Crump. "He had it comin' to him for goin' and stealin' you."

"He didn't steal me. He saved my life, and he was bringing me to Pelham Dutton's safari."

"Well, he's dead," said Crump, pushing Tarzan's limp body with his boot. "Come along with me. I'll take you to Dutton. Our camp's only about a mile from here."

"Aren't you going to do anything for him?" she demanded.

"I've done everything I wanted to with him already," said Crump with a laugh. "Come along now."

"Aren't you going to bury him?"

"I ain't no grave-digger. The hyenas and jackals'll bury him. Come along now. I can't waste no more time here. If there were any game around, that shot has scared it away by this time." He took her by the arm and started off toward camp.

"He said you were a bad man," said Sandra.

"Who said I was a bad man?"

"Tarzan."

"Well, I was too good for him."

As they departed, a pair of close-set, blood-shot eyes watched them from a concealing thicket, and then turned back to rest upon the body of Tarzan of the Apes.

Sandra and Crump reached camp before the others returned; and it was not until late in the afternoon that Dutton, the last of the three, came in with a small buck and a couple of hares.

When he saw the girl, he dropped his game and came running toward her. "Sandra!" he exclaimed, grasping both her hands. "Is it really you? I had about given up hope." His voice shook with emotion, and the girl saw tears in his eyes, tears of relief and happiness. "Who found you?" he asked.

"I found her," said Crump; "and I got that damned Tarzan guy, too. He won't never steal no more girls."

"He did not steal me," said Sandra. "I've told this man so a dozen times. He rescued me from a Waruturi village last night just as they were going to kill me; and this man shot him in cold blood and left him out there in the forest. Oh, Pelham, won't you come back with me, and bring some of the boys, and at least give him a decent burial?"

"I certainly will," said Dutton; "and I'll do it right away, if we can make it before dark."

"It's not far," said Sandra.

"Do you think you can find the place?" he asked.

"I don't know," she said.

"If it'll make you feel any better to bury him," said Crump, "I'll show you where he is; but I think it's damned foolishness. He's probably bein' et right now. It don't take hyenas long to locate a feed, or the vultures either."

"Horrible!" Exclaimed Sandra. "Let's start at once, Pelham."

Dutton gathered a half dozen of the black boys and, with Gantry leading the way, he and Sandra started out in search of Tarzan's body. Gantry and Minsky, curious to see the apeman close-up, accompanied them.

A half hour later they came to the water hole. Crump, who was in the lead, halted in his tracks with an oath and an exclamation of surprise.

"What's the matter?" demanded Dutton.

"The son-of-a-gun aint here," said Crump.

"You must have just wounded him," said Dutton.

"Wounded nothing! I shot him in the head. He was as dead as a doornail. It's sure damned funny what's become of him."

"Dead men don't walk away," said Gantry.

"Then something took him away," said Crump.

"He may be close by," said Sandra; and she called Tarzan's name aloud several times, but there was no reply.

"This is all very mystifying," said Dutton. "First you are captured by one Tarzan, Sandra, and then you are rescued by another Tarzan. I wonder which one was Tarzan, or if either of them were."

"The one I killed was Tarzan," said Crump. "I never seen the other one; but I knew this bloke all right."

"We might as well go back to camp," said Gantry. "There's no use hangin' around here."

"If I only knew," said Sandra.

"Knew what?" asked Dutton.

"Whether or not he's lying around somewhere near here only wounded, perhaps unconscious again and prey for the first prowling beast that comes upon him. He was so brave. He risked his life to save me."

"Well, he aint lying around wounded nowhere," said Crump. "He's dead. Some lion or somethin' drug him off; and, anyway, I don't see no sense in makin' such a fuss about a damn monkey-man."

"At least, he was a man and not a brute," said Sandra bitterly.

"If I'd knowed you had a crush on him, I wouldn't have shot him," said Crump.

"Shut up!" snapped Dutton. "We've taken all we're going to from you."

"So what?" demanded Crump.

"Don't," begged Sandra. "Don't quarrel. We've been in enough trouble without that. Take me back to camp, please, Pelham; and tomorrow we'll take our own safari and start back to father's."

"Yeah?" sneered Crump; "and Minsky and I'll come with you."

"We won't need you," said Dutton.

"Maybe you don't need us; but we're comin' with you anyway. I'm comin' to collect that reward."

"What reward?" demanded Sandra.

"Your father offered a reward of a £1000 for your return," explained Dutton, "and £500 for the capture, dead or alive, of the man who stole you."

"Then no one can collect either reward," said the girl. "You killed the man who rescued me; and the man who stole me is still at large."

"We'll see about that," growled Crump.

As the party made its way back to camp, savage eyes watched them. Among them was one pair of eyes that were neither savage nor unfriendly. They were the eyes of the man who thought he was Tarzan. The other eyes belonged to the great, shaggy, man-like apes which he called the servants of God.

After the party they were watching had disappeared toward their camp, the man and his companions came out into the open. The man was leading a black woman, a rope about her neck. He had been surprised to see Sandra Pickerall, for he had supposed that by this time she had been killed by the Waruturi. At sight of her his spirits had risen, for now again there was a chance that he might take back a white goddess with him to Alemtejo. He had been a little bit afraid to return again without one; so he had captured the Waruturi woman to take back as a slight peace-offering to da Gama.

After darkness had fallen on the jungle, the false Tarzan and his fierce band crept close to the camp of the whites where the man might watch and plan.

Sandra and Dutton sat before her tent discussing past events and planning for the future, while, out of earshot, Crump, Minsky, and Gantry spoke in whispers.

"I aint goin' to be done out of my share of that reward," Crump was saying, "and I gotta plan that ought to bring us twice as much."

"What is it?" asked Gantry.

"This guy, Dutton, gets killed accidental-like; then Minsky and I take the girl. You go back to the old man and tell him you put up a fight but we were too many for you. You tell him we let you go, so you could go back and report to him that we're holding the girl for £3000 ransom. There's three of us. We'll split it three ways. We each get a £1000, and you don't take no risk."

"I won't have nothin' to do with murder," said Gantry. "I gotta pretty clean record in Africa, and I aint gonna spoil it."

"That's because you ain't never been caught," said Crump.

"And I don't intend to get caught now," retorted Gantry, "and, anyway, this Dutton is a pretty good guy."

"There aint no use killin' him nohow," said Minsky. "Listen to me."

"Shoot," said Crump.

"After Dutton and the girl turn in tonight," continued Minsky, "Crump and I'll get our safari loaded up then we'll bind and gag you in your tent and steal the girl. When Dutton finds you in the mornin' you can tell him that we got the drop on you, but before we left with the girl we told you that her old man could have her if he would send £3000."

"Where to?" asked Gantry.

"I'm coming to that," said Minsky. "You know where old Chief Pwonja's village is on the Upindi River, don't you?"

"Yes," said Gantry.

"Well, that's where we'll take the girl. We'll wait there two months. If you haven't come with the ransom money by that time, we'll know what to do with her."

"But if I know where you are, that makes me a party to the whole business," said Gantry.

"No it don't," said Minsky. "Just tell 'em you had to take your choice between doin' what we tell you to do or gettin' killed and gettin' killed if you double-cross us. Knowin' Tom's reputation, they'll believe you."

"Your reputation doesn't smell so sweet," growled Crump.

"Well, between the two of us, our reputation ought to be worth £3000," said Minsky with a grin, "and them's pretty valuable reputations to have."

"But suppose you double-cross me?" demanded Gantry.

"Not a chance, Bill," said Crump. "You know I wouldn't never double-cross a pal."

But Gantry didn't know anything of the kind, nor did he know what was passing in the minds of these men, nor did they know what was passing in his mind. Neither Crump nor Minsky had the slightest intention of turning any of the £3000 over to Gantry; and, after it was once safely in their hands, Crump planned to kill Minsky and keep the entire amount; while Gantry hadn't the slightest intention of going to the village of Chief Pwonja on the Upindi River once he got his hands on the money. He had heard a lot about Hollywood, and he thought he could have a good time there with £3000. He could live there under an assumed name, and no one would be the wiser. And so these three precious characters laid their plans; and the moon crept behind a cloud; and Sandra and Dutton went to their respective tents.

The man who thought he was Tarzan watched and waited patiently. He noted the tent into which the girl had gone, and now he waited for the others to go to theirs. Finally, Gantry repaired to his tent; but Crump and Minsky were busy among the porters. The false Tarzan watched the blacks loading up their packs, and wondered; then he saw one of the whites go to the tent occupied by Gantry. In a few minutes he came out again and joined his companion. Presently the porters shouldered their packs and started off towards the west.

This was all very interesting. The man who thought he was Tarzan crept closer. He wished the two white men would go away with their porters; then he could easily go and get the girl; but they did not leave, and the man grew slightly impatient.

Sandra found it difficult to sleep. She was physically tired, but her mind and her nerves were dancing like dervishes. She could not drive from her thoughts the recollection of the murder of Tarzan. She still saw that magnificent figure crumpling in death, one instant so vital and alert, the next an inert lump of clay.

She loathed Crump for the thing that he had done; and now for weeks she would have to see him every day as they made the slow and laborious return trip to her father's camp; but she thanked God for Pelham Dutton. Without him, that return trip would be unthinkable. She tried to drive the death of Tarzan from her mind by thinking of Pelham. Her intuition told her that the man was very fond of her. He had never spoken a word of love; but there had been that in his eyes when he had greeted her this day that spoke far more eloquently than his words. She tried to evaluate her own feelings. Like any normal girl, she had had her infatuations and her little flirtations. Sometimes she had felt that they were love, but they had never lasted long enough for her to find out. She knew that she felt differently toward Pelham Dutton than she ever had toward any other man. It was a more solid, substantial, and satisfying feeling; and it was exhilarating, too. When he had grasped her hand at their meeting this day, she had had to deny a sudden impulse to creep into his arms and snuggle close to him for protection and sympathy; but that, she told herself, might have been a natural reaction after all that she had passed through. She might have felt the same way about any friend whom she liked and trusted.

She was still intent upon her problem when the flap of her tent was lifted and Crump and Minsky entered.

SEVEN . . Abducted

A GREAT BULL-APE had come along to the water-hole to drink; but, like all wild beasts who are the natural prey of Numa the lion or Sheeta the panther, he had reconnoitered first before coming into the open. From the concealment of a dense thicket, he had surveyed the scene; and presently he had seen the top of a bush near the water-hole move. There was no wind to move it; and immediately the anthropoid became suspicious. He waited, watching; and presently he saw a Tarmangani with a rifle raise himself just above the bush, take aim and fire. It was not until Tarzan pitched forward to the ground that the ape saw him and the girl with him. He waited until the girl and the man who had shot Tarzan had gone away; then he came out into the open and approached the body of the ape-man. He turned it over on its back and sniffed at it, making a little moaning noise in his throat; then he picked it up in his great, hairy arms and carried it off into the jungle.

* * *

Sandra Pickerall sat up on her cot. "Who are you?" she demanded. "What do you want?"

"Shut up," growled Crump. "We aint gonna hurt you, if you keep your trap shut. We're gettin' out of here, and you're comin' with us."

"Where's Mr. Dutton?" she demanded.

"If he's lucky, he's asleep. If you make any noise and wake him up, he's gonna get killed."

"But what do you want of me? Where are you going to take me?" she demanded.

"We're gonna take you some place where you'll be safe," said Crump.

"Why not tell her?" said Minsky. "Listen, lady, we're taking you where nobody won't find you until you old man comes across with £3000; and if you know what's good for you and this Dutton guy, you won't make us no trouble."

Sandra thought quickly. She knew that if she called for help, Dutton would come and he would be killed; for these were dangerous, desperate men whose situation would be affected little by an additional crime.

"Let me dress and get some of my things together," she said, "and I'll come quietly."

"Now you're talkin' sense," said Crump; "but just to be on the safe side, we'll wait for you while you dress."

The false Tarzan, followed closely by the servants of God, had crept close to the camp which lay unguarded, Crump having sent the askaris along with the porters.

As Crump, Sandra, and Minsky came from the girl's tent, the man who thought that he was Tarzan ran forward, closely followed by the great apes. Growling, striking, rending, the hairy beasts fell upon the two men, while their human leader seized the girl and dragged her quickly from the camp.

It was all over in a few seconds; but the noise had aroused Dutton, who came running from his tent, rifle in hand. In the flickering light of the campfire, he saw Crump and Minsky rising slowly to their feet, dazed and groggy, with blood streaming from several superficial wounds.

"What's the matter?" demanded Dutton. "What has happened?"

Minsky was the first to grasp the situation. "I seen something prowling around Miss Pickerall's tent," he said, "and I woke Crump and we come up here; then about a dozen gorillas jumped on us, but I seen a white man grab the girl and run off with her. It was that Tarzan again."

"Come on," said Dutton. "We've got to find her. We've got to follow them and take her away from them."

"It aint no use," said Crump. "In the first place, there's too many of them. In the second place, it's too dark. We couldn't never find their trail. Even if we did come up with them. We couldn't shoot for fear of hitting the girl."

"Wait 'til morning," said Crump.

"But there must be something we can do," insisted Dutton.

While the two were talking, Minsky had crept into Gantry's tent and unbound him, at the same time telling him what had happened. "He wants to go out lookin' for the girl," he concluded. "You go a little way with him and then make him come back, or let him go on alone for all I care; and in the meantime, we'll get the boys back into camp. If they come in while he's here, he'll sure be suspicious."

"O.K." said Gantry, and led the way out of his tent.

Dutton saw them coming, but Minsky forestalled his suspicions. "This guy is sure some sleeper," he said. "He slept through it all. I had to go in and wake him up."

"I'm going out to search for Miss Pickerall," said Dutton. "Are you men coming with me?"

"I'm not," said Crump, "because it wouldn't do no good."

"I'll go with you Mr. Dutton," said Gantry.

"All right then, come along," said the American, and started off in the direction that Crump had said the girl's abductors had taken her.

For a quarter of an hour they stumbled through the forest. Occasionally, Dutton called Sandra's name aloud; but there was no reply.

"It aint no use, Mr. Dutton," said Gantry, presently. "We can't find them at night, and even if we did stumble on 'em by accident, what could we do? Crump said there were ten or fifteen of 'em. We wouldn't stand a chance with 'em; and we wouldn't dare shoot for fear of hitting Miss Pickerall."

"I guess you're right," said Dutton despondently. "We'll have to wait until morning; then we'll take every man that we have a gun for, and follow them until we catch up with them."

"I think that's more sensible-like," said Gantry; and the two turned back toward camp. By the time they reached it, the porters and askaris were back; and there was no indication that they had been away.

When morning came it found the false Tarzan leading two women with ropes around their necks. One was a black Waruturi, the other was Sandra Pickerall. Trailing them were the shaggy, savage servants of God.

The two women were very tired, but the man forced them on. He knew that until they reached the thorn forest which lies at the base of the Ruturi foothills, he would not be safe either from the Waruturi or the white men whom he was sure would follow them; and he must not lose the white goddess again or da Gama would be very angry with him. It was a gruelling grind, with only occasional brief stops for rest. They had no food, for the man did not dare leave them alone long enough to search for it; but by nightfall, even the man who thought that he was Tarzan was upon the verge of exhaustion; and so they lay down where they were and slept until morning.

Ravenously hungry, but rested, they took up the march again at break of day; and, by noon, they came to the edge of the thorn forest.

There didn't seem to be a break in that interminable stretch of armed trees; but finally the man located a place where, by creeping upon all fours, they could avoid the thorns. They proceeded this way for a few yards, and then a trail opened up before them upon which they could walk erect.

After he had first captured her, the man had scarcely spoken for a long time, and he had been equally taciturn upon this occasion, speaking only when it was necessary to give orders; but when they had passed through the thorn forest and come out into the open, his attitude changed.

He breathed a sigh of relief. "Now we are safe," he said. "This time I shall bring da Gama the white goddess."

"Oh, why did you do it?" she said. "I have never harmed you."

"And I have never harmed you," he retorted; "nor do I intend to. I am doing you a great favor. I am taking you to be a goddess. You will have the best of everything that Alemtejo can give, and you will be worshiped."

"I am only an English girl," she said. "I am not a goddess, and I do not wish to be."

"You are very ungrateful," said the man.

Their trail wound up into the foothills; and ahead of them, Sandra could see a lofty escarpment, a formidable barrier, the Maginot Line, perhaps, of the Ruturi Range. Before they reached the escarpment they came to the narrow mouth of a gorge across which had been built a strong palisade. Sandra thought that this was the village to which she was being taken. A stream of clear water, sparkling in the sunlight, ran beneath the palisade and down through the foothills toward the great forest.

"Is that Alemtejo?" Sandra asked.

The man shook his head. "No," he replied. "It is the home of the guardians of Alemtejo. Alemtejo lies beyond."

Suddenly there burst upon the girl's ears a savage roar, which was followed by others in such tremendous volume that the ground shook.

Sandra looked around fearfully. "Lions!" she exclaimed. "Where can we go if they attack us?"

"They will not attack us," said the man, with a smile, "for they cannot get at us."

As they came closer to the palisade, the uprights of which were some six inches apart, Sandra could see beyond it into the widening gorge. Lions! Lions! She had never seen so many together before. They had caught the scent of man and they were coming toward the palisade growling and roaring.

At one end of the palisade a narrow trail ran up the side of the gorge. It was very steep; and it was only because rude steps had been hacked out of it that it could be scaled at all. Here the man took the rope from about Sandra's neck and turned her over to two of the apes, each of which seized one of her hands; then the man took the rope from about the neck of the black woman and urged her up the trail ahead of him. After the trail had topped the palisade it levelled off and ran along the side of the gorge. Below them, roaring lions leaped in an effort to reach them. The trail was narrow. A single misstep and one would be hurled down to the ravening lions below. The great apes edged along the trail, one in front of Sandra, one behind, clinging to her hands. The man and the black woman were just ahead.

Sandra could scarcely tear her eyes from the lions, some of them leaped so high and came so near to reaching them. The ape in front of her stopped; and as it did so she looked up to see why, just in time to see the white man push the black woman from the narrow trail.

There was a piercing scream as the woman hurtled to the lions below. There was a rush of padded feet and savage roars and growls below.

Sandra could not look. "You beast!" she cried. "Why did you do that?"

The man turned, a look of surprise upon his face. "I am no beast," he said. "The guardians of Alemtejo must eat."

"And I am next?" she asked.

"Of course not," he said. "You are a goddess."

They went on now in silence, the trail rising steeply to the far end of the canyon above which towered tremendous cliffs two or three thousand feet in height—sheer, almost vertical cliffs, over the summit of which fell a beautiful waterfall to form the stream which Sandra had seen running beneath the palisade.

Sandra wondered what they would do now. The mighty cliff blocked their progress forward. To their right was the unscaleable, vertical wall of the canyon; to their left, the gorge and the lions.

Where the trail ended at the foot of the cliff, it widened considerably for a short distance. Here the ape directly behind her dropped her hand and passed her and the man who had halted at the trail's end. The creature took the man's hand and commenced to ascend, helping the man from one precarious hold to the next. Sandra blenched from the implication, but the ape pulled her forward; and then he, too, commenced to ascend, dragging her after him.

There were crevices and tiny ledges and little hand-holds and foot-holds, and here and there a sturdy shrub wedged in some tiny crack. The girl was terrified, almost numb from fright. It seemed fantastic to believe that any creature other than a lizard or a fly could scale this terrific height; and below, the lions were waiting.

They came at last to a chimney, a narrow chute up which the apes wormed their way. Here they moved a little less slowly for the sides of the chimney were rough and there were occasional transverse cracks affording excellent foot and hand-holds.

Sandra glanced up. She saw the leading ape and the man above her. They had gained a little distance, for the man required less help than she. She did not dare look down. The very thought of it palsied her.

Up and up they climbed, stopping occasionally to rest and breathe. An hour passed, an hour of horror, and then a second hour. Would they never reach the top? The girl was suddenly seized with a horrid premonition that she would fall, that she must fall, that nothing could avert the final tragedy; yet up and up they made their slow, laborious way. Sandra's nerves were on edge. She wanted to scream. She almost wanted to jerk herself from the ape and jump, anything to end this unspeakable horror.

And then it happened! The ape placed his foot upon a jutting fragment; and, as he bore his weight upon it to lift himself to a new hand-hold, it broke away and he slipped back, falling full upon the girl. Frantically, blindly, she clawed for some support. Her fingers clutched a crevice. The ape struck her shoulder and bounded outward; but the impact of his body broke her hold and she toppled backward.

EIGHT . . Alemtejo

THE LIGHT OF THE SUN slanted through the foliage of ancient trees to mottle the sward of a small, natural clearing in the heart of the forest. It was quiet and peaceful there. The leaves of the trees whispered softly, purring to the caresses of a gentle breeze, here in the heart of an ancient forest as yet uncontaminated by the ruthless foot of man.

A dozen great apes squatted about something that lay in the shade at one side of the clearing. It was the lifeless body of a white man.

"Dead," said Ga-un.

Ungo, the king ape, shook his head. "No," he growled.

A she-ape came with water in her mouth and let it run upon the forehead of the man. Zu-tho shook the giant body gently.

"Dead," said Ga-un.

"No," insisted Ungo; and once again Zu-tho shook the ape-man gently.

Tarzan's lids fluttered and then opened. He looked dazedly up into the faces of the great apes. He looked about the clearing. His head ached terribly. Weakly, he raised a hand to a temple, feeling the caked blood of an ugly wound. He tried to raise himself on an elbow, and Ungo put an arm beneath him and helped him. He saw then that his body was splotched with dried blood.

"What happened, Ungo?" he asked.

"Tarmangani came with thunderstick. Bang! Tarzan fall. Tarzan bleed. Ungo bring Tarzan away."

"The she-Tarmangani?" asked Tarzan. "What became of her?"

"She go away with Tarmangani."

Tarzan nodded. She was safe then. She was with her own people. He wondered who had shot him, and why. He had not seen Crump. Well, every man's hand seemed to be against him. All the more reason why he should mend quickly and search out the impostor who was the cause of it all.

Tarzan recovered quickly from the effects of the wound which had creased his skull but had not fractured it.

One day when he felt quite himself again, he questioned Ungo. He asked him if he had ever seen another white man who went naked as Tarzan did. Ungo nodded and held up two fingers.

Tarzan knew that Ungo had seen such a man twice.

"With strange Mangani," added Ungo.

That was interesting—a man who said he was Tarzan, and who consorted with great apes.

"Where?" asked Tarzan.

Ungo made a comprehensive gesture that might have taken in half the great forest.

"Ungo take Tarzan?" asked the ape-man.

Ungo discussed the matter with the other apes. Some of them wished to return to their own hunting ground. They had been gone a long time, and they were restless; but at last they agreed to go with Tarzan, and the following day Tarzan of the Apes with his great anthropoid friends started toward the Ruturi Mountains.

* * *

When the body of the ape above her struck Sandra's shoulder, its course was sufficiently deflected so that it missed the other apes below it; but Sandra fell full upon the ape beneath her. Clinging precariously to scant holds, the beast grasped one of the girl's ankles; and though he could not retain his hold, his action retarded her fall, so that the ape below him was able to catch and hold her.

Hanging with her head down, the girl saw the body of the ape which had fallen hurtling downward to the gorge far below. Fascinated, she watched the grotesquely flailing arms and legs; but just before the body struck the ground she closed her eyes; then to her ears came the roars and growls of the great carnivores fighting over the body.

Looking down from above, the man, who had reached a ledge which afforded comparatively substantial footing, saw the predicament of the girl and the ape which held her. He saw that the great anthropoid could neither advance nor retreat, nor could the ape above him or the ape below him assist their fellow; while the girl, hanging with her head down, was absolutely helpless.

The horrified girl realized her plight, too. The only way that the ape could save himself was to relinquish his hold upon her. How long would it be before the great brute would surrender to the law of self-preservation?

Presently she heard the voice of the man above her. "I'm throwing a rope down to you. Tie it securely around your body. Sancho and I can pull you up then." As he spoke, he fastened together the ropes with which he had been leading the two women, and dropped one end down to the girl. With great difficulty, but as quickly as she could, Sandra fastened it securely about her body beneath her arms.

"I am ready," she said; and closed her eyes again.

The great ape, Sancho, and the man drew her slowly upward, inch by inch, in what seemed to her a protracted eternity of horror; but at last she stood on the tiny ledge beside her rescuer. She had been very brave through the hideous ordeal, but now the reaction came and she commenced to tremble violently.

The man placed a hand upon her arm. "You have been very courageous," he said. "You must not go to pieces now. The worst is over and we shall soon be at the summit."

"That poor ape," she said, shuddering. "I saw him fall all the way—all the way down to the lions."

"Yes," he said, "that was too bad. Fernando was a good servant; but those things sometimes happen. They are not without their compensations, however. The guardians of Alemtejo are none too well fed. Sometimes they kill one another for flesh. They are always ravenous."

Presently Sandra regained control of herself, and the ascent was resumed; but this time Sancho and the man retained hold of the rope.

Soon they came to a point where the chimney had been eroded far back into the cliff from the summit, so that it slanted upward at an angle of about forty-five degrees. By comparison with what had gone before, this was, to the girl, almost like walking on level ground; and in half an hour, during which they rested several times, they reached the summit.

Spreading before her eyes the girl saw a vast level mesa. In the near distance was a forest, and in the foreground a little stream wound down to leap over the edge of the cliff and form the waterfall to whose beauty she had been blinded by the terrors of the ascent.

The man who was called God let the girl lie down on the

green turf and rest. "I know what you have endured," he said sympathetically; "but it is over, and now you are safe. I am very happy to have brought you here safely." He hesitated, and the bewilderment that she had noted before was reflected in his eyes. "I am always happy when I am with you. Why is it? I do not understand."

"Nor I," said the girl.

"I did not want a goddess," he continued. "I did not want to go and look for one. When I found you, I did not want to bring you here. I know that you hate me, and that makes me sad; yet I am quite happy when you are with me. I do not think that I was ever happy before. I do not recall ever having been happy."

"But you did not have to bring me here," she said. "You could have stayed with my father's safari."

"But I did have to bring you here. Da Gama told me to bring you, and he would have been very angry had I not done so."

"You didn't have to come back here. I don't believe that you belong here. You are a very strange man."

"Yes. I am strange," he admitted. "I do not understand myself. You know," he leaned close to her, "I think that I am a little mad—in fact, I am sure of it."

Sandra was more than sure of it; but she didn't know what to say, and so she said nothing.

"You think I'm mad, don't you?" he demanded.

"You have done some very strange things," she admitted, "some very inconsistent things."

"Inconsistent?"

"Notwithstanding the fact that you stole me from my father, and later from my friends, you have been very kind and considerate of me; yet in cold blood and without provocation, you pushed that poor black woman to the lions."

"I see nothing wrong in that," he said. "All of God's creatures must eat. The Waruturi eat their own kind. Why should not the lions, who must live, too, eat Waruturi? You eat many of God's creatures that people have gone out and killed for you. Why is it wrong for the lions to eat one of God's creatures, but perfectly right for you to do so?"

"But there is a difference," she said. "That woman was a human being."

"She was a cruel and savage cannibal," said the man. "The little antelopes that you eat are harmless and kindly; so if either is wrong, it must be you."

"I am afraid neither one of us can ever convince the other," said Sandra, "and what difference can it make anyway?"

"It makes a lot of difference to me," he said.

"And why does it?" she asked.

"Because I like you," he said, "and I wish you to like me."

"Don't you think you are a little optimistic in believing I might like the man who stole me from my father and brought me to this awful place from which I may never hope to escape?"

"Alemtejo is not an awful place," he said. "It is a nice place to live."

"No matter how awful or how nice it is," she replied, "I shall have to stay here, for I never could go down over that awful cliff."

"I hoped you would learn to like Alemtejo and me, too," he said hopefully.

"Never," replied the girl.

The man shook his head sadly. "I have no friends," he said. "I thought perhaps at last I had found one."

"You have your people here," she said. "You must have friends among them."

"They are not my people," he said. "I am God, and God has no friends."

He lapsed into silence and presently they started on again in the direction of the forest that lay across the mesa. They followed the stream beside which was a well-worn trail that finally led into the forest, which they had penetrated for about half a mile when there suddenly burst before the astonished eyes of the girl a great castle set in a clearing. It was such a castle as she had seen in Abyssinia upon one of her father's former hunting expeditions, such a castle as the Portuguese, Father Pedro Diaz, built here at the beginning of the 7th Century.

Sandra had at that time read a great deal about Portugal's attempted colonization of Abyssinia, and was quite familiar with the details of that ill-fated plan. Many times she had heard her captor speak of da Gama; but the name held no particular significance for her until she saw this castle. Now the derivation of the other names he had used was explicable, such as Ruiz the high priest, and Fernando and Sancho, the apes—all Portuguese.

Now a new mystery confronted her.

NINE . . When the Lion Charged

DUTTON WAS UP before dawn the morning after Sandra's abduction by the false Tarzan and his servants of God. He searched for his boy, but was unable to find him. Mystified, he aroused the headman, telling him to arouse the other boys, get breakfast started, and prepare the packs for he had determined to take the safari along on the search for Sandra; then he aroused Gantry and the other two whites.

When dawn came, it was apparent that a number of the boys were missing, and Dutton sent for the headman. "What has happened?" he demanded. "What has become of the porters and askaris who are not in camp?"

"Bwana," said the headman, "they were afraid, and they must have deserted during the night."

"What were they afraid of?" demanded Dutton.

"They know that Tarzan and his apes came into camp last night and took the girl. They are afraid of Tarzan. They do not wish to make him angry. They are also afraid of the Waruturi, who are cannibals; and they are a long way from home. They wish to return to their own country."

"They have taken some of our provisions," said Dutton. "When we get back, they will be punished."

"Yes, Bwana," replied the headman, "but they would rather be punished at home than be killed here. If I were you, Bwana, I would turn back. You can do nothing in this country against Tarzan and the Waruturi."

"Tarzan's dead," said Crump. "I ought to know. I killed him myself. And as for the Waruturi, we can keep away from their villages. Anyway, we've got enough guns to keep them off."

"I will tell my people," said the headman; "but if I were you, I would turn back."

"I think he's got somethin' there," said Gantry. "I don't like the looks of it at all."

"Go back if you want to," said Crump; "but I ain't gonna give up that reward as easy as all that."

"Nor I," agreed Minsky.

"And I shall not give up," said Dutton, "until I have found Miss Pickerall."

It was not a very enthusiastic band of porters and askaris who started out with the four white men that morning. Dutton and Gantry headed the column, following the plain trail the apes had made, while Crump and Minsky brought up the rear to prevent desertion. The natives were sullen. The headman, ordinarily loquacious, walked in silence. There was no singing. The atmosphere was tense and strained. They marched all day with only one rest at noon; but they did not overhaul the girl and her captor.

Late in the afternoon, they surprised a lone warrior. He tried to escape, but Crump raised his rifle and shot him.

"A Waruturi," he said, as he examined the corpse. "See them filed teeth?"

"Holy smoke!" exclaimed Gantry. "Look at them gold ornaments. Why, the bloke's fairly loaded down with gold."

The blacks of the safari gathered around the corpse. They noted the filed teeth. "Waruturi," they murmured.

"*Mtu mla watu,*" said one, in a frightened voice.

"Yes," said the headman, "cannibals." It was evident that even he was impressed and fearful, nothwithstanding the fact that once in his own country he had been a noted warrior.

It was a glum camp they had that night; and in the morning when the white men awoke, they were alone.

Crump was furious. He went cursing about the camp like a madman. "The black devils have taken all of our provisions and most of our ammunition," he raved.

"That cannibal you killed finished them," said Gantry, "and I don't know that I blame them much. Them cannibals aint so nice. I think the boys had a hell of a lot more sense than we've got."

"You scared?" demanded Crump.

"I aint sayin' I'm scared, and I aint sayin' I aint," replied Gantry evasively. "I been in this country longer than you, Tom, and I've seen some of the things these cannibals do; and I've heard stories from old-timers all the way back to Stanley's time. There aint nothin' these cannibals won't do for human flesh. Why, they even followed Stanley's safari when his men were dying of smallpox and dug up the corpses and et 'em. I think we ought to turn back, men."

"And pass up that reward?" demanded Minsky.

"And abandon Miss Pickerall to her fate without even trying to find her?"

"We have tried to find her," said Gantry. "There aint one chance in a million that the four of us can get through this country alive. There aint one chance in ten million that we can rescue her, if we caught up with that Tarzan guy and his apes."

"Well, I'm going on," said Dutton. "The rest of you can do whatever you please."

"And I'm going with you," said Crump.

"You'd do anything for a few measly pounds," said Gantry.

"There's more than a few measly pounds in this," replied Crump. "You seen the gold on that warrior I killed yesterday, didn't you? Well, that reminded me about somethin' I heard a couple of years ago. That gold came from the Ruturi Mountains. It come out of there in lumps as big as your two fists. There's the mother lode of all mother lodes somewhere in them hills. If the Waruturi can find it, we can."

"I guess you'll have to go back alone, Gantry," said Minsky.

"You know damned well I could never get through alone," replied Gantry. "I'll go with you, but I get my share of the reward and any gold we find."

"There's a lot of funny stories about that gold," said Crump, reminiscently. "They say it's guarded by a thousand lions and two tribes that live way back in the Ruturi Mountains."

"Well, how do the Waruturi get it then?" asked Minsky.

"Well, those people back there in the mountains have no salt nor no iron. They send down gold to purchase them from the Waruturi, not very often but once in a while. The Waruturi buy salt and iron from other tribes, with ivory, for they know that sooner or later them guys will come down out of the mountains and bring gold."

"What makes you think you can find this here gold mine?" demanded Gantry.

"Well, it's up in the Ruturi Mountains and there must be trails leadin' to it."

"How about you, Dutton?" asked Gantry. "Are you in on it?"

"We have reason to believe that Miss Pickerall is being taken into the Ruturi Mountains. You are going there in search of your gold mine. As long as our routes lie in the same direction, we might as well stick together. I will agree to help you in your search, if you will agree to help me in mine. As long as we stick together, we have a better chance of getting through. Four guns are better than one, or two, or three."

"That makes sense," said Minsky. "We'll stick together."

"One thing we've got to do, no matter which way we go," said Gantry, "is eat! and we aint got nothin' to eat. We'll have to do some huntin' tomorrow."

Early the next morning the four men set out in different directions to hunt. Dutton went toward the west. The forest was open, and the going good. He hoped one of them would make a kill, so they could go on in search of Sandra Pickerall. He believed they were definitely on the trail of her abductors, and his hopes of finding her were high. He hated delay, even to hunt for food; but he had had to defer to the wishes of the others. After all, a man could not travel forever on an empty stomach.

He kept constantly alert for signs of game, but he was a civilized man with a background of hundreds of years of civilization behind him. His senses of smell and hearing were not keen. He could have passed within ten feet of the finest buck in the world, if the animal had been hidden from his sight; but there were other hunters in the forest with keen noses and ears.

Numa the lion had made no kill the night before. He was getting old. He did not spring as swiftly or as surely as in former days. He was missing the target all too often, sometimes only by a grazing talon. Today he was hungry. He had been stalking Dutton for some time; but the unfamiliar scent of the white man made him unusually wary. He slunk along behind the American, keeping out of sight as much as possible, lying suddenly flat and motionless when Dutton stopped, as he had occasionally, to listen and look for game.

There was another hunter in the forest with keener senses and a finer brain than either Dutton or Numa. Usha the wind had carried the scent spoor of both the man and the lion to his sensitive nostrils; and now, prompted more by curiosity than humanitarianism, he was swinging silently and gracefully through the trees upwind toward the two.

Dutton was commencing to believe there was no game in

the forest. He thought perhaps he was going in the wrong direction, and decided to strike off to the left to see if he could not find a game-trail in which was the spoor of some animal he might follow.

The lion was now fully in the open; and the instant Dutton stopped the great cat flattened itself on the ground; but there was no concealment, and as Dutton turned to the left his eye caught the tawny coat of the king of beasts. He looked to see what it was, and his heart sank. He had never killed a lion, but he had heard enough stories about them to know that even if your bullet pierced their heart they still might live long enough to maul and kill you. In addition to this was the fact that he knew he was not a very good shot. He started to back away toward a tree, with the thought in his mind that he might gain sanctuary among its branches before the lion reached him.

Numa rose very slowly and majestically and came toward him, baring his great yellow fangs and growling deep in his belly. Dutton tried to recall all he had heard about lion killing. He knew that the brain was very small and lay far in the back of the skull well protected by heavy bone. The left breast was the point to hit, just between the shoulder and the neck. That would pierce the heart, but the target looked very small; and even though the lion was only walking, it moved from side to side and up and down. Suddenly, backing up, Dutton bumped into a tree. He breathed a sigh of relief and glanced up. His heart sank, for the nearest branch was ten feet above the ground. He did not know it, but if the branch had been only four feet the lion could have reached him, had it charged, long before he could have climbed out of harm's way; for there are few things on earth swifter than a charging lion.

The great lion was coming closer. He seemed to grow larger as he came; and now he was growling horribly, his yellow-green eyes glaring balefully at his victim.

Dutton breathed a little silent prayer as he raised his rifle and took aim. There was a sharp report as he squeezed the trigger. The lion was thrown back upon its haunches, stopped momentarily by the impact of the bullet; then, with a hideous roar, it charged.

TEN . . Human Sacrifice

As SANDRA PICKERALL stood before the imposing castle of Alemtejo her hopes rose; for she felt that such an imposing edifice must be the abode of civilized men and women—people who would sympathize with her situation and perhaps eventually might be persuaded to return her to her own people.

She had expected to be taken to some squalid, native village, ruled over probably by a black sultan, where she would be reviled and mistreated by perhaps a score of wives and concubines. Her captor's insistence that she would be a goddess had never impressed her, for she was definitely convinced that the man was insane and thought his stories were but a figment of a deranged mentality.

"So this is the castle of Alemtejo!" she said, half aloud.

"Yes," said the man. "It is the castle of Cristoforo da Gama, the King of Alemtejo."

There was no sign of life outside the castle; but when her companion stepped forward and pounded upon the great gate with the hilt of his knife, a man leaned from the barbican and hailed him.

"Who comes?" he challenged; and then, "Oh, it is God who has returned."

"Yes," replied the girl's captor, "It is he whom the king calls God. Admit us, and send word to Cristoforo da Gama, the king, that I have returned and brought a goddess."

The man left the opening, and Sandra heard him calling to someone upon the inside of the gate, which presently swung slowly open; and a moment later Sandra and her captor filed into the ballium, while the servants of God turned back into the forest.

Inside the gate stood a number of chocolate-colored soldiers wearing helmets of gold and cuirasses of golden chain mail. Their brown legs were bare, and their feet were shod in crude sandals. All wore swords and some carried battle-axes, and others ancient muskets, the latter looking very impressive notwithstanding the fact that there had been no ammunition for them in Alemtejo for nearly four hundred years.

The ballium, which was wide and which evidently extended around the castle, was laid out with rows of growing garden truck, among which both men and women were working These, too, like the soldiers at the gate, were mostly chocolate-colored. The men wore leather jerkins and broad-brimmed hats, and the women a garment which resembled a sarong wound around their hips. The women were naked from the waist up. All showed considerable excitement as they recognized the man; and when, later, he and Sandra were being conducted across the ballium toward the main entrance to the castle, they knelt and crossed themselves as he passed.

Sandra was dumbfounded at this evidence that these people, at least, thought that her companion was a god. Maybe they were all insane. The thought caused her considerable perturbation. It was bad enough to feel that one might be associating with a single maniac, but to be a prisoner in a land of maniacs was quite too awful to contemplate.

Inside the castle they were met by half a dozen men with long gowns and cowls. Each wore a chain of beads from which a cross depended. They were evidently priests. These conducted them down a long corridor to a great apartment which Sandra immediately recognized as a throne-room.

People were entering this apartment through other doorways, as though they had recently been summoned, and congregating before a dais on which stood three throne chairs.

The priests conducted Sandra and her companion to the dais, and as they crossed the room the people fell back to either side and knelt and crossed themselves.

"They really take him seriously," thought Sandra.

After mounting the dais, three of the priests conducted the man, who thought he was Tarzan and who was called God, to the right-hand throne chair as one stood facing the audience chamber, while the other three seated Sandra in the left-hand chair, leaving the center chair vacant.

Presently there was a blaring of trumpets at the far end of the apartment. Doors were thrown wide, and a procession entered led by two trumpeters. Behind them was a fat man with a golden crown on his head, and behind him a double file of men with golden helmets and cuirasses and great, double-edged swords which hung at their sides. All these filed up onto the dais, all but the fat man with the crown, passing behind the three throne chairs and taking their stations there.

The man with the crown paused a moment before Sandra, half knelt and crossed himself; then he crossed over in front of the man whom they called God and repeated his genuflection before him, after which he seated himself in the center throne-chair.

The trumpets sounded again, and another procession entered the throne-room. It was led by a man in a long black robe and a cowl. From a string of beads around his neck depended a cross. He was much darker than most of the others in the apartment, but his features were not negroid. They were more Semitic and definitely hawk-like. He was Ruiz the high priest. Behind him walked the seven wives of the king. The women came and sat on buffalo robes and lion skins spread on the dais at the foot of the center chair. The high priest stood just below the dais, facing the audience.

When he spoke, Sandra recognized the language as a mixture of Portuguese and Bantu and was able to understand enough to get the sense of what the man was saying. He was telling them that now they had both a god and a goddess and that nothing but good fortune could attend them hereafter.

Ruiz stood behind a low, stone altar which appeared to have been painted a rusty-brown red.

For a long time, Ruiz the high priest held the center of the stage. The rites, which were evidently of a religious nature, went on interminably. Three times Ruiz burned powder upon the altar. From the awful stench, Sandra judged the powder must have consisted mostly of hair. The assemblage intoned a chant to the weird accompaniment of heathenish tom-toms. The high priest ocasionally made the sign of the cross, but it seemed obvious to Sandra that she had become the goddess of a bastard religion which bore no relationship to Christianity beyond the symbolism of the cross, which was evidently quite meaningless to the high priest and his followers.

She heard mentioned several times Kibuka, the wargod; and Walumbe, god of death, was often supplicated; while Mizimo, departed spirits, held a prominent place in the chant and the prayers. It was evidently a very primitive form of heathenish worship from which voodooism is derived.

All during the long ceremony the eyes of the audience were often upon Sandra, especially those of Cristoforo da Gama, King of Alemtejo.

At first, the rites had interested the new goddess; but as time wore on, she found them monotonous and boring. At first, the people had interested her. They evidently represented a crossing of Portuguese with blacks, and were slightly Moorish in appearance. The vast quantities of gold in the room aroused her curiosity, for, with the exception of herself and the man who was called God and Ruiz the high priest, everyone was loaded down with ornaments or equipment of gold. The wives of the king bore such burdens of gold that she wondered they could walk.

Sandra was very tired. They had given her no opportunity to rest; and she still wore the tattered garments that had been through so much, and the dirt and grime of her long trek. Her eyes were heavy with sleep. She felt her lids drooping, and she caught herself nodding when suddenly she was startled into wakefulness by loud screams.

Looking up, she saw a dozen naked dancing girls enter the apartment, and behind them two soldiers dragging a screaming negro girl of about twelve. Now the audience was alert, necks craned and every eye centered upon the child. The tom-toms beat out a wild cadence. The dancers, leaping, bending, whirling, approached the altar; and while they danced the soldiers lifted the still screaming girl and held her face up, upon its stained, brown surface.

The high priest made passes with his hands above the victim, the while he intoned some senseless gibberish. The child's screams had been reduced to moaning sobs, as Ruiz drew a knife from beneath his robe. Sandra leaned forward in her throne-chair, clutching its arms, her wide eyes straining at the horrid sight below her.

A deathly stillness fell upon the room, broken only by the choking sobs of the girl. Ruiz's knife flashed for an instant above his victim; and then the point was plunged into her heart. Quickly he cut the throat, and dabbing his hands in the spurting blood sprinkled it upon the audience, which surged forward to receive it; but Sandra Pickerall saw no more. She had fainted.

ELEVEN . . The Voice in the Night

AS THE LION CHARGED, Dutton fired again and missed; then, to his amazement, he saw an almost naked man drop from the tree beneath which he stood full upon the back of the lion momentarily crushing the great beast to the ground.

His attention now diverted from his intended prey, the great cat turned it upon the man-thing clinging to his back. A steel-thewed arm encircled his neck and powerful legs were locked beneath his belly. He reared upon his hind feet and sought to shake the creature from his back.

Dutton looked on, stunned and aghast. He saw the gleaming blade in the man's left hand plunge time and again into the beast's side, and he heard the former's growls mingle with those of the carnivore; and the flesh on his scalp crept. He wanted to help the man; but there was nothing he could do, for the swiftly moving, thrashing bodies rendered it impossible to use his rifle without endangering his would-be rescuer.

Soon it was over. The lion, mortally wounded by both rifle and knife, stood still for a moment on trembling legs and then fell heavily to the ground to lie quietly in death.

What happened next, Dutton knew would remain indelibly impressed upon his memory throughout his life. The victor rose from the body of his vanquished foe, and placing one foot upon the carcass raised his face toward the sky and voiced a hideous long-drawn-out scream. It was the victory-cry of the bull ape; though that, Dutton did not know. Then the man turned to him, the savage light of battle already dying in his eyes. "You are Pelham Dutton?" he asked.

"Yes," replied Dutton, "but how did you know?"

"I have seen you before; and the girl you are searching for told me your name and described you to me."

"And who are you?"

"I am Tarzan of the Apes."

"Which one?" demanded Dutton.

"There is only one Tarzan."

Dutton noticed the half-healed wound on Tarzan's temple. "Oh," he said, "you are not the one who stole Miss Pickerall. You are the one who rescued her, the one whom Crump shot."

"So it was Crump who shot me," said Tarzan.

"Yes, it was Crump. He thought it was you who had stolen Miss Pickerall."

"Mostly, however, he was thinking of the reward and his revenge. He is a bad man. He should be destroyed."

"Well, the law will probably get him eventually," said Dutton.

"I will get him eventually," replied Tarzan. He said it very simply, but Dutton was glad he was not Crump.

"What were you doing here in the forest alone?" demanded Tarzan.

"Hunting," replied the American. "The boys of our safari deserted us, taking all our provisions and equipment. We had no food; and so we started out in different directions this morning to hunt."

"Who are the others?" asked Tarzan, "Crump, Minsky, and Gantry?"

"Yes," said Dutton; "but how did you know their names?"

"The girl told me. She also told me that you are the only one of the four she trusted."

"I certainly wouldn't trust either Crump or Minsky," agreed Dutton, "and I'm not so sure about Gantry. He's been whispering with them too much lately, and his mind is more on the reward than it is on saving Miss Pickerall. You see, her father offered £1000 reward for her return."

"And £500 for me dead or alive," added Tarzan with a grim smile.

"Well, he offered that for the man who stole his daughter— a man who had told us he was Tarzan of the Apes."

"What have you done with Miss Pickerall while you are hunting?" Tarzan asked.

"She is not with us," said Dutton. "She was stolen again by a band of apes led by a white man. It must have been the same one who said he was Tarzan of the Apes."

"And are you looking for her?" asked the ape-man.

"Yes," replied Dutton.

"Then our paths lie in the same direction, for I am searching for the man who stole her. He has caused too much trouble already. I shall destroy him."

"You will come with us?" asked Dutton.

"No," replied the ape-man, "I do not like your companions. I am surprised that three such men, familiar with Africa, would take the chance they are taking for little more than £300 apiece, at the most £500—if they kill me, too—for I should say that without a safari, and only four guns, you haven't a chance on earth."

"They have another incentive," said Dutton.

"What is it?" asked the ape-man.

"A fabulous gold mine, which is supposed to lie in the Ruturi Mountains."

"Yes," replied Tarzan, "I have heard of it. I think there is no doubt that it exists, but they will never reach it."

"But you are planning on going into the Ruturi Mountains alone," said Dutton. "How do you expect to do it, if you think that four of us would fail?"

"I am Tarzan," replied the ape-man.

Dutton thought about that. The man's simple assurance that he could do what four men could not do impressed him. He was also impressed by the man's prowess as evidenced by his victory over the king of beasts in hand-to-hand-combat.

"I should like to go with you," he said. "You are going to find the man who stole Miss Pickerall; so if you find him I shall find her; and as you have rescued her once, I am sure you will help me to rescue her again. As for the other three, they are motivated solely by avarice. If there were no reward they would not turn a hand to save Miss Pickerall. If they find the gold mine, they will abandon their search for her."

"You are probably right," said Tarzan.

"Then I may come with you?" asked Dutton.

"How about the other three?" demanded the ape-man.

"They'll think something happened to me; but they won't even look for me. They really haven't much use for me."

"Very well," said the ape-man, "you may come with me if you can take it."

"What do you mean?" asked Dutton.

"I mean that you will be consorting with wild beasts. You will have to learn to think and act like a wild beast, which may be difficult for a civilized man. Wild beasts are not motivated by avarice, and but seldom by thoughts of vengeance. They have more dignity than man. They kill only in self-defense or for food. They do not lie or cheat, and they are loyal to their friends."

"You think a great deal of the wild beasts, don't you?" commented Dutton.

"Why shouldn't I?" asked the ape-man. "I was born and reared among them. I was almost a grown man before I saw another human being or realized that there were others of my kind. I was a grown man before I saw a white person."

"But your parents?" asked Dutton.

"I do not remember them," said Tarzan. "I was an infant when they died."

"I think I understand how you feel about men," said Dutton. "I sometimes feel the same way. I will come with you."

"Do you wish to go back to your camp first?" asked Tarzan.

"No. I have everything with me that I possess."

"Then come with me." Tarzan turned and started off toward the north.

Dutton followed along, wondering what lay in store for him with this strange creature. He felt a certain confidence in him; but perhaps that was because he had felt no confidence at all in his three companions. Presently they came to an open glade through which ran a stream. Dutton involuntarily stopped and fingered his rifle, for squatting around the glade were a dozen huge anthropoid apes, great, shaggy, savage looking fellows. He saw them rise, growling, as Tarzan approached them; then he heard the man speak in a strange tongue, and he saw the apes relax as they answered him.

Tarzan turned and saw that Dutton had stopped. "Come on," he said. "Let them smell of you and get acquainted with you. I have told them that you are my friend. They will not harm you; but they will not be friendly. Just leave them alone, especially the shes and the balus."

"What are balus?" asked Dutton.

"The babies, the young ones," explained Tarzan.

Dutton approached, and the great apes came and sniffed him and touched him with their horny hands. Suddenly one of them grasped his rifle and tore it with his hand. Tarzan spoke to the ape, which then relinquished the rifle to him. "They don't like firearms," he said. "I have told them that you would only use it to obtain food or to defend the tribe. See that that is all you use it for."

"Speaking of food," said Dutton, "do you suppose I could get a shot at something around here? I am nearly famished. I have had nothing but a little fruit in the last couple of days."

Tarzan raised his head and sniffed the air. "Wait here," he said. "I'll bring you food." And with that he swung into a tree and disappeared in the foliage.

Dutton looked about at the great savage beasts around him, and he did not feel any too happy. It was true that they ignored him, but he recalled stories he had heard about the bulls going berserk for no apparent reason. He fell to thinking, and suddenly a doubt assailed him. Here was a white man who consorted with apes. A white man, accompanied by a band of apes, had stolen Sandra. Could there be two such creatures in the jungle? Could there be such a coincidence? He commenced to doubt Tarzan's sincerity, and he looked about him for some sign of Sandra. He got up and walked about, peering behind bushes. There could be some clue. There was always a clue in story books—a handkerchief, a bit of cloth torn from a garment, a dainty footprint. He found none of these; but still he was not satisfied, and he was still wandering about in the vicinity of the clearing when Tarzan returned, a small antelope across one shoulder.

Tarzan cut the hind quarter from his kill and tossed it to Dutton. "You can build a fire?" he asked.

"Yes," said the American.

"Cut off what you want to eat now," said the ape-man; "and save the rest for tomorrow."

"I'll cook enough for you too," said Dutton. "How much can you eat?"

"Cook your own," said Tarzan, "and I will take care of myself." He butchered the carcass, cutting off several pieces; then he carried the viscera downwind and tossed it among the bushes. When he came back he handed pieces to each of the apes, which, while generally herbivorous, occasionally eat flesh. They squatted down where they were, Tarzan among them, and tore at the raw meat with their fangs, growling a little as they did so.

Dutton was horrified, for the man was eating his meat raw as the beasts did and growling as they growled. It was horrible. He grew more and more apprehensive. He wouldn't have given a lead nickel for his chances now.

Night had fallen as they completed their meal. "I shall be back presently," Tarzan said to Dutton. "You may lie down anywhere and sleep. The apes will warn you if any danger threatens"; then he told Ungo to see that no harm befell the man. Ungo grunted.

* * *

It had been late when the last of the three men returned to camp. None of them had had any luck. Each had gathered and eaten some fruits and nuts; but it was flesh they craved, good red meat to give them strength.

"I wonder where the toff is," said Gantry. "I thought we'd find him here when we got back."

"I don't give a damn where he is," said Crump. "The sooner I don't never see him again, the better I like it. I aint got no use for them blighters."

"He weren't such a bad lot," said Gantry.

"He was like all the rest of 'em," said Minsky. "You know what they all think of us; think we're a lot of scum and treat us like it. I hate all the damn bourgeoisie. They're part and parcel of the capitalistic system, takin' the bread out of workers' mouths, grindin' down the proletariat under the iron heel of imperialism."

"Rot!" said Crump. "I aint got no use for 'em myself, but I got less use for a damned bolshie."

"That's because you're a creature of capitalism," said Minsky. "You probably even belong to a church and believe in God."

"Shut up," said Crump.

"Say," commenced Gantry, more to change the subject than anything else, "did you guys hear a scream this afternoon?"

"Yes," said Minsky. "What was it do you suppose?"

"I heard it, too," said Crump. "It sounded sort of like —well—I don't know what."

"Sounded like a banshee to me," said Gantry. "The natives have told me though that bull-apes sometimes scream like that when they have made a kill."

"I'm turnin' in," said Gantry.

"O.K." said Crump. "I'll stand guard for four hours; then I'll wake you. Minsky will follow you. Keep up the fire and see that you don't go to sleep while you're on watch, either of you."

Minsky and Gantry lay down upon the ground, while Crump threw some more wood on the fire and squatted beside it. It was very quiet. Beyond the limits of the firelight there was a black void. Their whole universe was encompassed in that little circle of firelight.

Crump was thinking of what he could do with the ransom money and the riches he hoped to bring back from the fabulous Ruturi gold mine, when the quiet was suddenly broken by a voice coming out of the darkness.

"Go back," it cried. "Go back to your own country. Go back before you die."

Gantry and Minsky sat up suddenly. "What the hell was that?" whispered the latter in a frightened voice.

TWELVE . . The King Comes

WHEN SANDRA REGAINED CONSCIOUSNESS, she was lying on a couch covered with buffalo skins; Ruiz the high priest was leaning over her mumbling a lot of incomprehensible mumbo-jumbo; while looking on were four native women and a lad of about nineteen. The natives were staring at her, wide-eyed and frightened; and when they saw that her eyes were open, they dropped upon their knees and crossed themselves.

Ruiz nodded. "I have brought her back from heaven, my children," he said. "Attend her well. It is the command of Cristoforo da Gama, King of Alemtejo, and of Ruiz the high priest;" then he crossed himself and left the room.

The natives were still kneeling. "Get up," she said; but they did not move. She tried again in Swahili and they stood up. "Who are you?" she asked in the same tongue.

"Your slaves," replied the lad.

"Why do you look so frightened?" she demanded.

"We are afraid," he said, "to be so near a goddess. Do not kill us. We will serve you faithfully."

"Of course, I won't kill you. What made you think I would?"

"The high priest kills many natives and throws them to the guardians of Alemtejo. A goddess would want to kill more than a high priest, would she not?"

"I do not want to kill anyone. You need not be afraid of me. What is your name?"

"Kyomya," said the lad. "How may we serve you, goddess?"

Sandra sat up on the edge of the cot and looked around. The room was large and rather bare. It was simply furnished with a table and several benches. The floor was covered with skins of buffalo and lion. The windows were two narrow, unglazed embrasures. At one side of the room was a large

63

fireplace. As long as she was a gooddess, she thought, she might as well make the most of it.

"Kyomya," she said.

"Yes, goddess."

"I want a bath, and some clean clothes, and food. I am famished."

The natives looked surprised, and it occurred to Sandra that perhaps they felt that a goddess should not be famished—that she shouldn't need food at all.

Kyomya turned to one of the girls. "Prepare a bath," he said; and to another, "Go, and fetch food. I will bring raiment for the goddess."

After awhile the three girls took her to an adjoining apartment where water was being heated over a charcoal brazier. They undressed her, and two of them bathed her while a third combed her hair. Sandra was commencing to feel very much like a goddess.

Presently Kyomya came with raiment; and it was raiment, not just ordinary clothing or even apparel. Evidently Kyomya had never heard of Emily Post, for he walked into the room without knocking and seemed perfectly oblivious of the fact that Sandra was naked. He laid the raiment on a bench, and walked out; and then the three girls clothed her. Her undergarment was a softly tanned doeskin, over which they fitted a skirt of fine gold mesh that was split down one side. Two highly ornamented golden discs supported her breasts. The straps of her sandals were studded with gold, and there was a golden ornament for her hair, as well as anklets, armlets, and rings of the same metal.

She felt that her garment was just a little more than décol-leté; but inasmuch as none of the women she had seen in Alemtejo had worn anything at all above the waist, she realized that she was quite modestly gowned; and anyway who was she to say how a goddess should dress? Even Schiaparelli might not know that.

The bath had refreshed and rejuvenated her, and now, richly clothed, she could almost feel that she was a goddess; but try as she would, she could not erase the memory of the frightful scene she had been forced to witness in the throne room. As long as she lived she would see that pitiful figure on the altar and hear the screams and the racking sobs.

In the next room, food was laid out for her on the table;

and while she ate, the five slaves hovered about, handing her first this and then that.

There were fresh fruits and vegetables, and a stew she later learned was of buffalo meat. It was highly seasoned and entirely palatable, and there was a heavy wine which reminded her of port, and strong black coffee. Evidently the King of Alemtejo lived well. It was no wonder he was fat.

Just as she was finishing her meal, the door was thrown open to the blaring of trumpets; and the king entered.

Sandra Pickerall was quick-witted; otherwise she might have arisen and curtsied; but in the same instant that she knew it was the king, she remembered she was a goddess; and so she remained seated.

The king advanced, half bent a knee and crossed himself.

"You may be seated," said Sandra. She spoke in Swahili, hoping the king might understand; and she spoke quickly before he could sit down without permission. It was just as well to put a king in his place from the start.

Da Gama looked a little surprised, but he sat down on a bench opposite her; then he ordered her slaves to leave the apartment.

"Kyomya will remain," she said.

"But I sent him away," said the king.

"He will remain," said Sandra the goddess, imperiously.

Da Gama shrugged. Evidently he had found a real goddess. "As you will," he said.

Poor Kyomya looked most uncomfortable. Beads of sweat stood on his forehead, and the whites of his eyes showed all around the irises. It was bad enough to be constantly risking the displeasure of a goddess without actually displeasing a king.

"You have been well attended?" asked da Gama. She felt naked beneath his gaze.

"Quite," she said. "My slaves are very attentive. I have been bathed and clothed, and I have eaten. Now all I desire is rest," she concluded, pointedly.

"Where did God find you?" he asked.

"Where does one find a goddess?" she retorted.

"Perhaps he spoke the truth, then," said the king.

"What did he say?" she asked.

"He said you were sent directly to him from heaven."

"God knows," she said.

"You are very beautiful," said the king. "What is your name?"

"My name is Sandra," she replied; "but you may call me either Holy One or Goddess. Only the gods may call me Sandra."

"Come, come," he said. "Let's be friends. Let's not stand on ceremony. After all, I am a king. You may call me Chris, if you wish to."

"I do not wish to," she said. "I shall call you da Gama; and by the way, da Gama, how did you get that name?"

"I am Cristoforo da Gama, King of Alemtejo, a direct descendant of the first Cristoforo da Gama, brother of Vasco da Gama."

"What makes you think so?" said Sandra.

"What makes me think so!" exclaimed the king. "It is recorded in the history of Alemtejo. It has been handed down from father to son for four hundred years."

"Unless my memory has failed me or history lies, Cristoforo da Gama, the brother of Vasco da Gama, was defeated by the Moslems and killed with all his four hundred and fifty musketeers. At least, da Gama was put to death."

"Then your history lies," said the king. "Cristoforo da Gama escaped with half his musketeers. A horde of Moslems chased them south, until finally they found sanctuary here. They made slaves, and prospered; and during the first hundred years they built this castle, they, and their descendants; but the Moslems camped on the other side of the valley and constantly made war upon Alemtejo. Their descendants are still there and still making war upon us, except during those times when we are making war upon them."

"Alemtejo," said the girl. "The name is very familiar, yet I cannot place it."

"It is the name of the country from which the da Gamas originally came," said the king; and then she recalled.

"Oh, yes," she said, "it is a province in Portugal."

"Portugal," he said. "Yes, that is mentioned in our history. I used to think I would go out and conquer the world and find Portugal; but it is very pleasant here in Alemtejo; so why should I go out among naked barbarians whose food is probably atrocious?"

"I think you are quite wise," said Sandra. "I am sure it would not be worth your while to conquer the world. Oh, by the way, have you conquered the Moslems across the valley yet?"

"Why, of course not," he said quickly. "If I conquered them, we would have no one to fight; and life would be very dull."

"That seems to be the general feeling all over the world," she admitted; "and now, da Gama, you may go. I wish to retire."

He looked at her through half-closed eyes. "I'll go this time," he said, "but we are going to be friends. We are going to be very good friends. You may be a goddess, but you are also a woman."

As the king left Sandra's apartment he met Ruiz in the corridor. "What are you doing here, Chris?" demanded the high priest.

"There you go again," whined da Gama. "Anybody'd think you were king here. Isn't this my castle? Can't I go where I please in it?"

"I know you, Chris. You keep away from the goddess. I saw the way you looked at her today."

"Well, what of it?" demanded da Gama. "I am king. Do I not sit on a level with God and his goddess? I am as holy as they. I am a god, as well as a king; and the gods can do no wrong."

"Rubbish!" exclaimed the high priest. "You know as well as I do that the man is no god and the woman no goddess. Fate sent the man down from the skies—I don't know how; but I'm sure he's as mortal as you or I; then you got the idea that by controlling him you could control the church, for you know that who controls the church controls the country. You were jealous of me, that was all; then you conceived the idea of having a goddess, too, which you thought might double your power. Well, you have them; but they're going to be just as useful to me as they are to you. Already, the people believe in them; and if I should go to them and say that you had harmed the girl, they would tear you to pieces. You know, you don't stand any too well with the people, Chris, anyway; and there are plenty of nobles who think that da Serra would make a better king."

"Sh-h-h," cautioned da Gama. "Don't talk so loud. Somebody may overhear you. But let's not quarrel, Pedro. Our interests are identical. If Osorio da Serra becomes King of Alemtejo, Pedro Ruiz will die mysteriously; and

Quesada the priest will become high priest. He might even become high priest while I am king."

Ruiz scowled, but he paled a little; then he smiled and slapped the king on the shoulder. "Let us not quarrel, Chris," he said. "I was only thinking of your own welfare; but then, of course, you are king, and the king can do no wrong."

THIRTEEN . . Captured by Cannibals

GANTRY HAD NOT SLEPT WELL the night the voice had come to them out of the darkness. It had spoken but the once; yet all through an almost sleepless night, Gantry had heard it again and again. It was the first thing he thought of as he awoke. Crump and Minsky were already on their feet.

"We'd better be movin'," said the former. "We got to kill us some meat today."

"What do you suppose it was?" said Gantry.

"What do I suppose what was?" demanded Crump.

"That voice last night."

"How should I know?"

"It spoke Swahili, but it didn't sound like no native voice," continued Gantry. "It told us to turn back or we'd be killed."

"How's a voice gonna kill you?" demanded Minsky.

"There was somethin' back of that voice," said Gantry, "and I don't think it was human."

"Bunk!" exclaimed Crump. "Come along. We got to be movin'."

"Which way you goin'?" demanded Gantry.

"Where do you suppose I'm goin'? To the Ruturi Mountains, of course."

"Then I aint goin' with you," said Gantry. "I know when I've had enough, and I'm goin' back."

"I always thought you were yellow," said Crump,

"Think whatever you damn please," said Gantry. "I'm goin' back."

"That's O.K. by me," said Crump. "One less to divide the reward with."

"Dead men can't spend no reward," said Gantry.

"Shut up!" said Minsky.

"And get the hell out of here," added Crump.

"You bet I will," said Gantry, swinging his rifle to the hollow of his arm and starting off toward the south.

Just before he passed out of sight, he turned and looked back at his two former companions. Did he have a premonition that he was looking for the last time on the faces of white men?

Two days later the drums of the Waruturi bid the tribesmen to a feast.

* * *

When Tarzan went away, leaving Dutton alone with the apes, the American had tried to sleep; but his mind had been so active in reviewing his recent experiences and in an attempt to solve some of the baffling enigmas that had presented themselves, that he had been unable to do so.

The more he thought about Tarzan and the apes, the more convinced he became that Tarzan was the man who had abducted Sandra; but why had Tarzan befriended him? Perhaps he was only pretending, so he could hold him for ransom, also, as Dutton was commencing to believe was the real reason for the abduction of Sandra, unless the man were, in fact, an irresponsible madman.

In either event, he could gain nothing by remaining with Tarzan, and his only hope of rescuing Sandra would depend upon his reaching her before Tarzan did.

Finally, he decided that his only recourse was to escape from the madman and make his way alone to the Ruturi Mountains; and inasmuch as Tarzan was away, he might not find a better time.

Dutton rose and walked slowly away from the apes. Those which were not already asleep paid no attention to him; and a moment later he had plunged into the forest.

Occasional glimpses of the stars aided him in maintaining his direction. A small pocket-compass which he carried would serve the same purpose during the day; so he groped his way through the dark night, a helpless thing only half appreciating his helplessness; and while he moved slowly on toward the north, Tarzan of the Apes swung back to the camp of the great apes where he quickly discovered the absence of the American. Assuring himself that he was not in the immediate vicinity, he called Dutton's name aloud, but there was no response; then he awakened the apes and questioned them. Two of them had seen the tarmangani walk out of the camp. Further than that, they knew nothing. Another might have thought they had disposed of the man and were lying to

Tarzan, for it had been obvious that they had not liked him and had not wished him around; but Tarzan knew that beasts do not lie.

Tarzan is seldom in a hurry. Time means nothing to the denizens of the jungle. Eventually, he knew, he would catch up with the impostor and destroy him; but it was immaterial whether it was today, tomorrow, or next month; and so it was that Tarzan and his great shaggy companions moved in a leisurely fashion toward the Ruturi Mountains, the apes foraging for food while the man lay in dreamy indolence during the heat of the day.

Very different, however, it was with the young American straining to the limit of his physical ability to reach his goal before he was overtaken by the man whom he now believed to be mad and a menace both to him and Sandra Pickerall.

During his brief experience in Africa, Dutton had always had someone with him with far greater experience upon whom to depend, with the result that he had not profited greatly by his weeks in the jungle; and so was pathetically vulnerable to surprise and attack, blundering on seemingly oblivious to the dangers which surrounded him.

Elephants, rhinoceroses, buffaloes, leopards, and lions do not hide behind every bush in Africa. Men have crossed the whole continent without seeing a single lion; yet there is always a chance that one of these dangerous beasts may be encountered, and he who would survive must always be on the alert.

To move quietly is to move with greatest safety, for noise appraises a keen-eared enemy of your approach, at the same time preventing you from hearing any noise that he may make.

His mind occupied with his problems, it is possible he was unaware of the fact that he often whistled little tunes or sometimes sang; but if he was not aware of it, there came a time when a dozen dusky warriors were. They stopped to listen, whispering among themselves; and then they melted into the undergrowth on either side of the trail; and when Dutton came abreast of them they rose up, encircling him and menacing him with threatening spears. He saw the golden ornaments and the filed teeth, and he knew, from what he had heard, that he was confronted by Waruturi cannibals. His first thought was of recourse to his rifle; but almost simultaneously he realized the futility of offering resistance, and a moment later the temptation was entirely removed by a villainous-looking warrior who snatched the weapon from him.

They handled him pretty roughly then, striking him and poking him with their spears; and then they bound his hands behind his back and put a rope about his neck and led him along the way he had just come in the direction of the trail which turned east toward the Waruturi village.

Tarzan was coming north along the trail the Waruturi were following south with their captive; but he was moving very slowly, so slowly that there was little doubt that the savages would turn from this trail onto the one leading to the east before he reached the intersection; this close was Dutton to possible succor.

Dutton realized the seriousness of his situation. He knew he had been captured by cannibals. How could he persuade them to release him? He could think only of a reward; but when he saw the golden ornaments with which they were adorned he realized the futility of that. Threats would be of no avail, for they were too far back in the hinterland to have knowledge of the white man's law or of his might; and even if there were some argument by which he could persuade or coerce them into releasing him, how was he to transmit it to them in the few words of Swahili with which he was familiar?

There was, however, one hope to which to cling. He knew that the mad Tarzan was coming north toward the Ruturi Mountains. He had saved Sandra Pickerall from these same cannibals. Might he not, then, find the means to rescue him, also; or had he sacrificed any right to expect this because of his desertion of Tarzan?

With these troubling thoughts was Dutton's mind occupied, when presently the Waruturi turned to the left upon a new trail; then the American's heart sank, for now there was no hope at all.

The warrior who took Dutton's rifle from him was very proud of his acquisition and was constantly fingering it and playing with it, until inadvertently he cocked it and squeezed the trigger. As the muzzle happened to be pointing at the back of the man in front of him at the time, the result was most disastrous to the man in front; but, fortunately for him he was never aware of his misfortune since the projectile passed cleanly through his heart.

This accident necessitated a halt and a long palaver, during which Dutton was struck several times with the haft of a spear by the brother of the man who had been killed, and would have been killed himself had not the leader of the party intervened in his behalf, wisely realizing that it was much easier to get beef home on the hoof than to carry it.

More time was occupied in the construction of a rude litter on which to carry the body of the dead buck back to the village, for, from being a boon companion, he had now suddenly been transformed into a prospective feast; thus considerably assuaging their grief. I think you can probably see how that would be yourself, if you were very hungry and your rich uncle died, and you could not only inherit his wealth but also eat him into the bargain; but of course that is neither here nor there, as you probably haven't a rich uncle, and if you have, the chances are that he will leave his money to a foreign mission in the nature of a bribe to Saint Peter to let him in.

Before resuming the march, the Waruturi unbound Dutton's hands and made him carry one end of the litter upon which lay the corpse.

FOURTEEN . . "Then the Door Opened"

AFTER THE KING left the apartment, Sandra's slaves prepared her for bed. They snuffed out the cresset which had lighted the room; and Kyomya lay down across the threshold of the doorway which opened onto the corridor. Faintly and from far away came the roars of the guardians of Alemtejo, as the exhausted girl sank into slumber.

The following day passed without incident. She saw neither the king nor Ruiz. In the afternoon, she walked out, attended by Kyomya and guarded by two warriors. She left the castle upon the opposite side from which she had entered, and there she saw a village of thatched huts extending from the castle wall out onto the plain. Here lived the common people, the tillers of the soil, the herdsmen, the artisans, and the common soldiers. There were many of them; and all whom she passed, knelt and crossed themselves. Kyomya was very proud.

At one side of the village were large corrals in which were many buffalo. At sight of them, Sandra expressed surprise, for she had always understood that the African buffalo was a savage, untamable beast, perhaps the most dangerous of all the wild animals of the Dark Continent.

"But what can they be used for?" she asked Kyomya.

"These are the war buffalo," he told her. "We have many more, but the herders have them out on pasture now. These, the warriors of Alemtejo use when they go to war with the Moslems."

"The Moslems! Who are they?" demanded Sandra.

"They are my people," said Kyomya. "We live in a village in the mountains across the plain. Sometimes we come down to raid and kill, or steal the buffalo of Alemtejo. We are Gallas, but they call us Moslems. I do not know why. We also use buffalo when we make war. I was with a raiding party of Gallas three rains ago. It was then that I was captured by the Alemtejos and made a slave."

"They keep all these buffalo just for war?" asked Sandra.

"For their meat, too; for their milk and their hides. They are very valuable to the Alemtejos and to us. My father owned many buffaloes. He was a rich man. When the Alemtejos kill a buffalo, they waste nothing; for what they do not use themselves, they throw over the great cliff to the lions."

Kyomya told her many things that day. He told her of the rich gold mine in the mountains beyond the valley. "Why, the gold is so plentiful that it is taken out in great pieces sometimes as large as your head, and all pure gold. Often, a bull buffalo cannot carry the load that is collected in a single day; but it is not easy for the Alemtejos to get the gold, because the mine is in the mountains not far from our village; and almost always when they come to work the mine, we attack them."

That evening after dinner there was a knock upon Sandra's door. It surprised her, because no one had ever knocked before. Those who wished to do so had merely entered without any formality.

To her invitation to come in, the door opened; and the man who was called God entered the apartment.

When she saw him she thought immediately of the king's visit, and jumped to the conclusion that this man had come for the same purpose.

He looked around the room. "They seem to have made you comfortable," he remarked.

"Yes," she replied. "Now, if they will only leave me alone."

"What do you mean?" he asked.

She told him about the visit of the king and his advances, more to warn him than for any other purpose.

"The beast!" he said. He laid a hand gently upon hers. "Can you ever forgive me for bringing you here?" he said. "I am so sorry; but I always seem to be confused. I don't know just why I do things, except that they tell me to, and I have to do what they say; but why should I? Am I not God? Yes, I am God; and yet I have wronged you, the one person in the world whom I would not have wished to wrong; but perhaps I can make it up to you," he said suddenly.

"How?" she asked.

"By trying to take you away from here," he replied.

"Would you do that?" she asked.

"I would do anything for you, Sandra. There is nothing in all the world I would not do for you."

There was that in his tone of voice and in his eyes that

warned her; and yet, suddenly and for the first time, she was not afraid of him.

They talked for a half hour, perhaps; and then he bade her goodnight and left; and now she wondered about him more than before. His remorse for having abducted her was, she felt, quite genuine; and it was quite obvious that he really believed he had been compelled to do it, that he could not at that time have refused to obey the king. Now she knew it was different. He was no longer obsessed by any false sense of loyalty.

She sat thinking of him after he had left, and wondering about him, for he unquestionably presented an enigma for which she could find no solution. Sandra discovered that her interest in the man was growing. At first, she had actively hated him for what he had done; and then it had become only resentment for his act; and then, as she saw more of him, her attitude toward him had changed, until now she found herself trying to make excuses for him. It angered her a little, because she could not understand this attitude of hers; nor could she find any sane explanation of his attitude toward her. She tried to analyze some of the things he had said to her, and she always came back to the same assumption; yet it was so ridiculous she could not harbor it. But was it ridiculous that this man should love her? They had been together much. She knew she was an attractive girl; and she was the only white woman he had seen during all these weeks. She was sure that whatever his sentiments toward her might be, they were not dictated by purely brute passion. He had had her absolutely in his power for a long time, and he had never offered her even the slightest incivility.

The girl wondered—wondered if this strange man loved her, and of a sudden she wondered what she thought about it.

After the man who was called God left her apartment, he walked toward his own, which was at the far end of the same corridor. As he was entering the doorway of his apartment, he happened to glance back along the corridor just as Ruiz entered it from another, transverse corridor.

The man watched the priest. He saw that he was going in the direction of Sandra's room; then he entered his own apartment and closed the door.

Sandra's slaves were disrobing her for the night, when the door of the apartment opened and Ruiz the high priest entered.

"What do you mean," the girl demanded, "by entering my apartment without permission?"

A sneering smile curled Ruiz' lips. "Don't put on airs with me," he said. "If you can entertain God in your apartment at night, you can certainly entertain his high priest. For your information, I will tell you that I have my spies everywhere in the castle; and one of them told me that God was here and that he had been here a long time. He must just have left before I came."

"Get out of here," she commanded.

"Come, come, let us be friends," he coaxed. "If you are good to me, you can have just about anything you want in Alemtejo; and you and I can rule the country."

"Get out," she repeated.

He came toward her, leering. "Don't touch me," she cried, shrinking away.

He seized her arm and drew her toward him, while Kyomya and the four slave-girls cowered, terrified, in a corner.

"Help me, Kyomya," cried the girl.

Kyomya hesitated a moment, and then he leaped to his feet and ran toward the couch. Ruiz heard him coming and turned to meet him, still clinging to Sandra. With his free hand he struck the boy heavily in the face and knocked him to the floor.

Kyomya leaped to his feet. "Leave my goddess alone," he cried. "Leave her alone, or I'll kill you;" and then he leaped full upon the priest.

Ruiz had to relinquish his hold upon Sandra then, and grapple with the Galla slave; but the advantage was all upon the side of the high priest, for almost instantly he whipped a knife from beneath his robe and plunged it deep into the heart of Kyomya. One of the slave-girls in the corner shrieked, for she was in love with Kyomya.

Sandra tried to elude Ruiz and reach the door; but he seized her again and dragged her back to the couch. She struck at him and kicked him, but he forced her slowly back; and then the door opened.

FIFTEEN . . "Set the White Man Free!"

THE GREAT APES searched for food: plantain, banana, tender shoots, and occasionally a juicy caterpillar. Tarzan arose and stretched. "Come," he said to them. "Now we go."

He started slowly along the trail toward the north, when there came distinctly to his ears the report of a rifle. That would be Dutton, he thought. Was he hunting? Or was he in trouble? The shot came from the direction in which Tarzan was going; and he decided to investigate. Scaling a nearby tree, he swung away in a direct line toward the point from which the report of the rifle shot had come.

The Waruturi moved on in the direction of their village, urging Dutton on with blows and prodding him occasionally with the point of a spear.

The white man had had no sleep the night before, and practically no food all day; and he staggered beneath the burden and the blows. Several times he was on the point of throwing down his load and attacking his tormentors, feeling that it was better to die at once than to suffer further maltreatment only to be tortured and killed in the end. He wished now that he had put up a fight while he still had his rifle; but at that time he had felt there might be some hope; now he knew there was none.

Two natives carried the front end of the litter, while he carried the rear alone. Suddenly, one of the blacks screamed and pitched forward upon his face, an arrow protruding from between his shoulders. The other blacks stopped in consternation and gathered around, looking in all directions for the author of the attack.

"The white man," cried the brother of the man who had been shot. "He has done this." And he raised his spear to thrust it through Dutton's heart; and then he, too, collapsed, an arrow in his own.

The blacks were thoroughly mystified and frightened now; and then a voice came to them, saying, "Set the white man free."

The blacks conferred for a moment; and then decided to push on with their prisoner, abandoning their three dead, for three were too many for them to carry while a mysterious enemy lurked somewhere near them.

Again came the voice. "Set the white man free." But now the blacks pushed on almost at a run.

A third man fell, pierced by an arrow; and once again the voice demanded that they liberate their prisoner.

This was too much for the blacks; and a moment later Dutton stood alone in the trail, while the Waruturi fled toward home.

A moment later, Tarzan of the Apes dropped into the trail near Dutton. "You should never wander away from camp," he said. "It is always dangerous. The apes will protect you." He thought that Dutton had walked away from the camp the previous night and been captured by the Waruturi.

"You certainly came just in time," said Dutton. "I don't know how I can ever repay you." He realized that Tarzan did not guess he had run away from camp, and he decided that the safest procedure was to remain the captive of the madman until he found Sandra; then wait for a reasonably good opportunity for escape to present itself.

Early the next morning they reached the thorn forest, where Tarzan found little difficulty in locating the secret entrance, and a little later they reached the gorge and saw the guardians of Alemtejo.

The apes had not been over-enthusiastic about negotiating the narrow trail above the lions; but at Tarzan's insistence they had done so; and at last they all reached the foot of the towering precipice.

Tarzan looked up toward the summit, and his keen eye quickly detected indications that the cliff had been scaled recently. He turned to Dutton. "It looks rather formidable, doesn't it?" he said.

"Yes," replied the American; "but it's not impossible. I have done a lot of mountain climbing in northwest Canada, the United States, and Switzerland; but I wouldn't advise you to attempt it."

"Oh, I think I'll try it," said the ape-man.

"But do you think you can make it?" demanded Dutton.

"I think so. The man I am looking for and the girl must have come this way; and if they could do it, I think I can."

"You mean Miss Pickerall went up that awful place?" demanded Dutton.

"Well, she's not here; and unless she fell to the lions, she went up, because I have followed her spoor all the way—she, and the man who calls himself Tarzan, and the apes that were with them."

"The apes must have gone back," said Dutton, "just as yours will have to."

"Why will they have to go back?" asked Tarzan.

"Why, they're too big and heavy and clumsy to scale this cliff."

For answer, Tarzan spoke to Ungo. The ape grunted something to the other apes; then he started the ascent, followed by his fellows.

Dutton was amazed at their agility and the speed with which they ran up the vertical cliff; and a moment later he was still more amazed when Tarzan followed them, equally as agile, he thought, as the anthropoids; and then, a moment later, he realized that the ape-man was more agile and far swifter.

With a shake of his head, Dutton followed; but he could not keep up with them. They not only climbed more rapidly than he, but they did not have to stop and rest, with the result that they reached the summit a full hour before he. Dutton threw himself on the sward, panting. Tarzan looked at him, the suggestion of a smile touching his lips.

"Well, the apes and I managed to make it, didn't we?" he said.

"Don't rub it in," said Dutton, smiling ruefully. "I already feel foolish enough."

After Dutton had rested, they started on again. The trail, lying clear to the eyes of the ape-man, stretched across the plain toward the forest. Presently they heard shouts and screams in the distance ahead of them.

"I wonder what that is?" said Dutton.

The ape-man shook his head. "It sounds like a battle," he said.

"But I don't hear any shots," said Dutton.

"There are still people in the world who kill one another with primitive weapons," explained the ape-man. "They are using bows-and-arrows and, of course, probably spears."

"How do you know they are using bows and arrows?" asked Dutton.

"I can hear the twang of the bow strings," replied the ape-man.

Dutton made no reply, but he was all the more convinced that the man was crazy. How could anyone identify the twang of a bowstring through all that tumult and at such a distance?

"What had we better do?" asked Dutton.

"We'll have to go and see what is happening. Maybe your girl friend is in trouble; and somewhere ahead the man I am looking for is waiting to die."

"You are going to kill him?" demanded Dutton.

"Certainly. He is a bad man who should be destroyed."

"But the law!" exclaimed Dutton.

"Here, I am the law," replied Tarzan.

As they entered the woods the sounds grew in volume, and there was no doubt in the mind of either but that a battle was raging a short distance ahead of them. They advanced cautiously; and the sight that met their eyes when they reached the far edge of the strip of forest filled even the phlegmatic ape-man with wonder, for there stood a huge medieval castle, its barbican and its walls manned by brown warriors in golden helmets and golden cuirasses hurling darts and javelins and boulders down upon a horde of screaming, cursing, black warriors armed with bows and arrows and lances.

"Amazing!" exclaimed Dutton. "Look at them on that scaling ladder. They are certainly heroic, but they haven't a chance. And look what's coming now!" He pointed.

Tarzan looked and saw a tower the height of the wall surrounding the castle. It was filled with black warriors, and it was being dragged toward the wall by a team of twenty buffaloes, urged on by screaming blacks wielding heavy whips.

So engrossed were the two men with watching the thrilling incident occurring before their eyes that neither of them, not even the keen-sensed Tarzan of the Apes or his shaggy fellows, were aware that a detachment of black warriors had discovered them and was creeping upon them from the rear. A moment later they charged with savage yells.

Momentarily, they overwhelmed the two men and the apes; but presently the great anthropoids and the Lord of the Jungle commenced to take a toll of their attackers; but in the melee two of the apes were killed and Dutton captured.

Against such odds, Tarzan was helpless; and as the blacks, reinforced by another detachment, charged him, he swung into the trees and disappeared.

SIXTEEN . . The Plan That Failed

THE NIGHT PRECEDING the capture of Dutton by the black Galla warriors, the man whom da Gama called God had entered his room and closed the door. For a moment he stood there in indecision. He had seen Ruiz the high priest turn down the corridor in the direction of Sandra's apartment. He recalled what the girl had told him about the king's visit; and he was troubled. Presently he reopened the door and stepped back into the corridor. It would do no harm to investigate. As he walked slowly along the corridor, he heard a woman scream; and then he broke into a run.

As he opened the door of Sandra's apartment he saw Ruiz choking the girl and forcing her back upon the couch. He saw the body of Kyomya lying on the floor and the four terrified slave-girls huddled in a corner.

An instant later a heavy hand fell upon the shoulder of the high priest. It jerked him from his victim and whirled him about to stand face to face with the man he called God. As Ruiz recognized his assailant, his features became contorted with rage.

"You fool!" he cried, and losing all control whipped a knife from beneath his robe. A futile gesture.

The man who thought he was Tarzan grasped the other's wrist and wrenching the knife from his grasp hurled it across the room. He spoke no word, but whirling Ruiz around again he seized him by the scruff of the neck and propelled him toward the door which still stood open. There he gave him a push and planted a kick that sent the man sprawling out into the corridor; then he closed the door.

He turned to the girl. "I am glad I came in time," he said.

"I can never repay you," she said; "but what will they do to you now?"

The man shrugged. "What can they do to God?" he demanded.

82

Sandra shook her head. "But you are not God—try to realize that. Ruiz and da Gama don't think you are a god or that I am a goddess. They are just using that to fool the people for political reasons."

"What makes you think so?" he asked.

"Poor Kyomya overheard them talking in the corridor last night."

"I am not surprised," he said. "I never did think I was God; but I didn't know who or what I was; and when they insisted that I was God, it seemed easier to agree. I am glad I'm not. I'm glad you are not a goddess."

"But who *are* you?" she asked.

"I don't know." She saw the strange, puzzled expression return to his face. Suddenly he brightened. "I am Tarzan of the Apes. I had almost forgotten that."

"But you are not Tarzan of the Apes," she said. "I have seen him; and you do not even look alike except that you are about the same size, and neither of you wears enough clothes."

"Then who am I?" he asked, hopelessly.

"But can't you recall anything of your past life?" she asked.

"Only that I was here and that they told me I had come out of the sky, and that I was God, even when I insisted I was Tarzan."

"But how were you dressed when you came? Your clothing should certainly give some clue as to your origin and, perhaps, to your identity."

"I was dressed just as you see me now—just a loincloth—and I carried my knife and my bow and arrows."

"It is absolutely inexplicable," said the girl. "People just don't happen like that, fully grown; and how in the world did you get to my father's camp? It must have been over a hundred miles from here."

"When da Gama sent me out to look for a goddess, the servants of God went with me to help me and protect me; and we kept on going until we found you."

"You went through all that dangerous country without a safari, without provisions, and still without a mishap?"

"We met lions and leopards, but they never attacked us. Perhaps they were afraid of the apes; and the few natives we saw certainly were. As for food, the apes took care of themselves and I had no trouble getting game. I am an excellent shot with bow and arrow, as Tarzan of the Apes should be."

"I wish I knew," she said; and he seemed to sense what she meant.

"I wish I did," he said.

Presently he dragged Kyomya's body into the corridor, and closed the door; then he gathered up some of the skins from the floor and laid them across the doorway.

"What are you doing?" asked Sandra.

"I am going to sleep here," he said. "I would not dare leave you alone again."

"Thank you," she said. "I am sure that I shall sleep better, knowing you are here." It did not even occur to her to wonder at the change that had come over her feelings in respect to this man whom she had so recently feared and hated and thought mad.

While Alemtejo slept, black warriors came down from the mountains beyond the plain and gathered in the forest behind the castle; and they were still there the next morning when the four slaves served breakfast for two in the apartment of Sandra Pickerall.

While she and the man ate, they discussed their plans for the future. "I think we should try to get out of here," said the man. "You will never be safe in the castle of da Gama."

"But how can we leave?" she asked.

"To everyone but da Gama and Ruiz, we are still a god and a goddess. I have left the castle whenever I pleased and no one has attempted to stop me."

"But where can we go?"

"We can go back the way we came, back to the camp of your father," he said.

"But that cliff!" she exclaimed. "I never could go down that awful place. I know that I should fall."

"Don't worry about that," he said. "I'll see that you get down, and we'll take the servants of God along to help and to protect us on the way."

The girl shuddered. "I don't believe I can do it," she said.

"You are going to do it, Sandra," he stated emphatically. "I brought you here, and I am going to take you away."

"But if you and I go out of the castle with all those apes, some one will suspect something."

"They are probably already out in the forest," he told her. "There is where they spend most of their time. When we are safely in the woods, I will call them and they will come."

"Very well," she said. "Let's get it over."

"We'll go out the front gate," he said, "and then circle the castle to the woods. If they look for us they will think we are in the village."

They made their way down the stairway, across the ballium, and to the front gate without difficulty. It was there that Sandra was sure they would be halted; but as they approached the gate, the soldiers knelt and crossed themselves, and the two passed out into the village.

In a leisurely manner, so as not to arouse suspicion, they circled the castle and entered the forest.

"That was miraculously easy," said the girl. "It is something to be a goddess."

"It will all be as easy as that," he assured her. "You are practically safe now;" but even as he spoke, a horde of black warriors surrounded them.

Resistance was useless. They were outnumbered fifty to one. The man thought quickly. He knew these were ignorant savages and thought that if the slightly more civilized inhabitants of Alemtejo believed that he was god, perhaps these Gallas might believe it, too.

"What do you want of us?" he demanded, imperiously. "Do you not know that I am God and that this is my goddess?"

It was evident the blacks were impressed, for the leader drew aside with several of his lieutenants and they whispered together for a few minutes. At last, the leader came back and stood before them.

"We have heard of you," he said.

"Then stand aside and let us go," commanded the man.

The black only shook his head. "We will take you to the Sultan," he said. As he ceased speaking, a great shouting and tumult came from the opposite side of the castle. "They have come!" he exclaimed. "Now we must attack from this side;" then he turned to one of his lieutenants.

"Take ten warriors and conduct these two to the Sultan."

SEVENTEEN . . The White Slave

MINSKY WAS HUNGRY for good red meat; but when he saw a buck and would have shot it, Crump stopped him. "Don't you know we're in the Waruturi country, you fool?" he said. "Do you want to tell 'em where they'll find some good meat for their cooking pots, and have a whole pack of the devils down on us in no time?"

"I thought you was such a friend of old Chief Mutimbwa," said Minsky. "You was tellin' us how chummy you and him was, and how we couldn't get through the Waruturi country without you. You was always goin' to his village and takin' him presents."

"That was so they wouldn't beef about our goin' along with 'em," said Crump. "I didn't want to have no trouble if I didn't have to. I never been to the Waruturi village and I never seen old Mutimbwa but once; and then I was with a safari with twenty guns. I give him some grade goods for some goats and chickens, and he give us permission to pass through his country; but the real reason was he was afraid of them twenty guns. If he caught us two alone, we could just kiss ourselves goodby; so I guess you'll have to go on eatin' bananas and plantain for awhile—unless you like grasshoppers and white ants."

Minsky thought this all over very carefully, and the more he thought of it the more bitterly he resented what Crump had done to him. He would not have entered the Waruturi country for any amount of gold, had he not believed that Crump was on friendly terms with Mutimbwa. Now he was in a trap from which he might never escape; but if he ever did, the first thing that he would do would be to kill Crump. He brooded on this constantly as they slunk stealthily through the dark forest.

At last, they came to open country; and across a rolling

tree-dotted plain they saw the Ruturi range looming purple in the distance.

"Well," said Crump, "that was not so bad."

"What was not so bad?" demanded Minsky.

"We are out of the Waruturi country. They're forest people. There isn't one chance in a thousand we'll run into any of 'em out here; and there's the mountains where the gold is, and there's the thorn forest."

"And there's some men," said Minsky, pointing toward the right.

The two men drew back into the concealment of the forest, and watched a file of men coming from their right up near the edge of the thorn forest. They counted fifteen walking in single file.

"Them's not Waruturi," said Crump.

"What they wearin'?" demanded Minsky. "They got on shiny coats and hats."

"Five of 'em carryin' packs on their heads," commented Crump. "It looks like a safari all right, but it's the doggonest lookin' safari I ever seen."

"Well, they're probably white men; and as long as they ain't Waruturi, they'll probably be friendly. Let's go on out and see."

Shortly after Crump and Minsky came out into the open, they were discovered by the other party, which halted; and the two men could see that every face was turned toward them. They were still too far separated to distinguish details. They could not tell whether the men were white or black; but they naturally assumed there were white men in the safari, which did not continue the march but stood waiting for their approach.

"They aint white," said Minsky presently.

"And they aint blacks, either," replied Crump, "only four of the porters—they're blacks all right. The fifth one looks like a white man. Say, those guys have got on golden shirts and hats."

"Their skins are light brown like they was tanned," said Minsky. "Maybe they are white men, after all."

"I don't care what color they are," said Crump. "They sure know where that gold mine is, and wherever they go we're goin' with 'em."

Presently a voice hailed them. "I say," it called out. "Do you understand English?"

Crump and Minsky saw that it was the white porter who was speaking. "Sure, we understand English," replied Crump. "Why?"

"Because then you can understand me when I tell you to get the hell out of here before these people get hold of you. Get word to the nearest English official that Francis Bolton-Chilton is a prisoner in the Ruturi Mountains."

"You mean they'll try to kill us if they get hold of us?" asked Crump.

"No," replied the man, "they'll make a slave of you as they have of me."

"We could rescue that guy," said Minsky. "Those other guys ain't got no guns. We could pick 'em off one by one." He started to raise his rifle.

"Hold on," said Crump. "We're lookin' for that gold mine, ain't we? Well, here's a way to find where it is. Let 'em make slaves of us. After we've located the mine and got what we want, we can always escape."

"That's takin' a hell of a chance," said Minsky.

"I've taken worse chances than this for a few hundred pounds of ivory," replied Crump. "Are you with me, or are you goin' back through the Waruturi country alone?"

"I'll stick," said Minsky. "As long as they don't kill us, we always got a chance. I wouldn't have none down there in the Waruturi country alone." He was thinking what a fool he was to have come with Crump in the first place. He was more than ever determined now to kill his partner when he no longer needed him. Crump was already moving forward again toward the strangers, and Minsky fell in at his side.

"Go back," shouted Bolton-Chilton. "Didn't you understand what I told you?"

"We're comin' along, buddy," replied Crump. "We know what we're doin'."

As they reached the safari they were surrounded by six or eight brown warriors wearing golden cuirasses and helmets. One of the warriors addressed them in a language they did not understand but which was faintly familiar.

Bolton-Chilton sat down on his pack. "You're a couple of blooming asses," he said.

"What they sayin'?" asked Crump. "I can't understand their lingo."

"They're telling you that you're prisoners and to throw

down your guns. If you want to talk to them, try Swahili. They understand it, even way up here."

"Those guys from Zanzibar covered a lot of ground in their day," said Crump. "I aint never been nowhere in Africa yet that someone didn't understand Swahili." He turned then and spoke to the warrior who had addressed him. "We're friends," he said. "We want to come along with you to your village and talk with your chief." He spoke in Swahili.

The warriors closed in upon them. "You will come to Alemtejo with us," said the leader; then their guns were snatched from their hands. "You will come as slaves. Pick up two of those loads. The other slaves need a rest."

"Didn't I tell you you were blooming asses?" said Bolton-Chilton.

"He's got your number all right, Crump," said Minsky, disgustedly.

"Hold on here," said Crump to the leader of the party. "You aint got no right to do that. I tell you we're friends. We aint no slaves."

"Pick up those two loads," said the warrior, pointing and at the same time he prodded Crump with his spear.

Grumbling profanely, Crump hoisted one of the packs to his head; and then Minsky picked up the other one.

"They aint no use beefin'," said Crump. "Aint we gettin' nearer to that gold mine all the time? And, anyway, these packs aint so heavy."

"It's not the weight," said Bolton-Chilton. "It's the bally humiliation—carrying packs for half-breeds!" he concluded, disgustedly.

"Where are they headin' for?" asked Minsky. "Where are they takin' us?"

"To Alemtejo," replied the Englishman.

"What sort of place is that?" asked Crump.

"I've never been there," explained Bolton-Chilton. "About two years ago I was captured by Gallas, who live in a village overlooking the plain where Alemtejo is. I have seen the castle of Alemtejo from a distance, but I have never been there. A couple of weeks ago I was coming down from a mine with a bunch of other slaves and an escort of Galla warriors, when we ran into these bounders. There was a bit of a scrimmage and I was captured. The Gallas didn't treat me so bad. They're pretty good primitives; but I've heard some beastly stories about these Alemtejos. They've some sort of heathenish religion with human sacrifices and that kind of stuff, and the Gallas say they feed people to a bunch of captive lions."

"You been here two years," asked Minsky, "and never had no chance to escape?"

"Not a chance," said Bolton-Chilton.

"You mean we got to stay here all the rest of our lives?" demanded Minsky.

"I've been here two years," said the Englishmen, "and there hasn't been a waking minute of that time that I haven't been looking for a chance to escape. Of course, I wouldn't have known in what direction to go; and I probably would not have lived to get through the Waruturi country; but a man had better be dead than to spend a long life in slavery, only eventually to die of starvation or be fed to lions. When a slave of the Gallas becomes unable to work through sickness or old age, they quit feeding him; so he just naturally dies of starvation; and the Alemtejos, I am told, throw their old slaves to the lions. If you two had done as I asked you, you would not have been captured and I might have been rescued."

"That was this wise guy," said Minsky, tossing an angry look at Crump. "We could have rescued you ourselves, with our two guns; but no, this fellow has to find a gold mine."

Bolton-Chilton laughed a little bitterly. "He'll find his gold mine all right," he said; "but he'll work in it under the hot sun like a galley slave. Before he's through with it, he'll hate the sight of gold."

"I'll take the chance," said Crump, "and I won't stay here no two years neither."

They walked on in silence for some time; and presently the leader of the detachment deployed his men and the slaves with intervals of a few feet between the men.

"What's the idea?" asked Minsky of the Englishman. "We aint goin' into battle, are we?"

"They spread out like this," replied Bolton-Chilton, "so they won't leave a well defined path to a secret entrance they have through that thorn forest there."

Again silence for some time; and again it was broken by Minsky. "What's in these here packs?" he asked.

"Salt and iron," replied the Englishman. "We brought down gold to the Waruturis to trade for salt and iron. Both the Gallas and the Alemtejos do it several times a year."

When they had passed through the thorn forest, they saw a well defined trail leading straight in the direction of a towering escarpment; but the Alemtejo warriors did not follow this path. Instead, they turned to the left, deployed once again, and moved off almost at right angles to the path.

"The Gallas say that trail there is mostly to fool people," said Bolton-Chilton. "Sometimes the Alemtejos do scale that cliff, but it's difficult and dangerous. The other way onto the plateau is much easier; but they try never to take the same way twice and never to march in single file, except in one place where there is but one way to ascend. If you ever expect to escape, watch very carefully where we go and take a note of every landmark. I did it coming down and I am going to do it again going up."

"Then there is a chance to escape?" asked Minsky.

"There is always hope," replied Francis Bolton-Chilton.

EIGHTEEN . . King of All the Apes

THE BATTLE OF ALEMTEJO, little more than a swift raid, was soon over. The defenders repulsed the blacks who would have scaled the wall on the forest side of the castle; and when the enemy bore down upon the village on the opposite side, the great gates of the castle swung open and Osorio da Serra led a sortie of twenty chariots drawn by charging buffaloes and filled with warriors. In a solid line they bore down at a mad gallop upon the Galla warriors, who turned and fled after setting fire to a few grass-thatched huts and making off with the several peasants they had captured to take into slavery.

Osorio da Serra did not pursue the fleeing blacks, for such was not according to the rules of warfare that long years of custom had evolved.

These sudden raids were in the nature of a game that was played between the "Moslems" and "Christians" and they had their rules, which were more or less strictly observed. They served to give a little spice to life and an outlet to the natural exhibitionism of man. The Alemtejos liked to wear cuirass and helmet and carry obsolete muskets for which there was no ammunition. The Gallas loved their warpaint and their feathers and their spears. The prototype of each is to be found in the sabre-clanking Prussians and the loud-mouthed, boastful, European dictator.

So the victorious Osorio da Serra rode back triumphantly through the gates of Alemtejo, and the fat king writhed with jealousy that was fuel to his hate.

Tarzan of the Apes watched the battle on the forest side of the castle, an interested spectator, only to see it end as quickly and as unexpectedly as it had begun. He saw the black warriors gather up their dead and wounded and take them away, together with their scaling ladders and a great tower drawn by twenty buffaloes which had served no purpose whatever.

Tarzan wondered at the futility of it all and the useless

waste of men and material—the silly expenditure of time and effort to no appreciable end; and his low estimate of man became still lower. Tarzan had already made his plans, and this silly encounter had interfered with them. He intended to present himself boldly at the gate of the castle and expect that hospitality which he knew to be common among civilized people; but he must wait now until the following day, because he knew that the attack on their fortress would leave the defenders nervous and suspicious.

Tarzan's reveries were presently rudely interrupted by a medley of growls and savage grunts, among which he recognized an occasional "kreeg-ah!" and "bundolo!" Thinking that the apes of Ungo were preparing to fight among themselves, he aroused himself and swung through the trees in the direction from which the disturbance had come. "Kreeg-ah" is a warning cry, and "bundolo" means to kill or to fight to kill—either one may be a challenge. When he came above the spot where the apes were congregated, he found Ungo and his fellows facing a band of strange apes. Each side was endeavoring to work itself up to a pitch of excitement that must eventually lead to battle.

Tarzan, poised above them, saw the seriousness of the situation at a glance. "I kill," growled Ungo; and a great bull ape facing him bared his fangs and repeated the challenge.

"I am king of the apes of Ungo," screamed Ungo.

"I am Mal-gash, king of the apes," cried the other.

The ape-man dropped from the tree between the two great brutes and faced Mal-gash. "I am Tarzan, king of all the apes," he said.

For a moment, Mal-gash and his fellows, the servants of God, were perplexed, for the man went naked except for a G-string just as the other, whom they knew as Tarzan, had gone; and he gave the same name—Tarzan, which means white-skin in the language of all the apes and the monkeys.

Mal-gash lumbered back to his fellows and they jabbered together for a few moments; then he turned and came back toward the ape-man. "Tarmangani not Tarzan," he said. "Mal-gash kill."

"Tarzan kill," growled the ape-man.

"Kreeg-ah!" screamed Mal-gash, and leaped for the man with huge, flailing arms.

The other apes watched, making no move to take part in the combat, for when king ape meets king ape they must decide the issue between themselves, and upon its result depends the sovereignty of one or the other. If Mal-gash defeated Tarzan, either by killing him or causing him to surrender, then Mal-gash might truly proclaim himself king of all the apes. Of course, he had no doubt but that he was already all of that; but it would be good to feel his fangs sink into the throat of this puny and presumptuous man-thing. As he rushed forward he sought to seize Tarzan; but as his great arms closed, Tarzan was not between them, and Mal-gash felt a blow on the side of his head that sent him reeling momentarily. With a savage roar he turned upon the ape-man again; and again he missed a hold as his agile opponent ducked beneath his outstretched arms and, turning, leaped upon his back. A steel forearm passed around his short neck and closed tightly beneath his chin. He tore at the arm with both hands, but repeated blows behind one of his ears dazed and weakened him.

The watching apes were restless, and those of Mal-gash suddenly apprehensive for they had expected a quick victory for their king. As they watched, they saw the ape-man turn suddenly and bend forward; and then they saw the huge body of Mal-gash thrown completely over his antagonist's head and hurled heavily to the ground. As he fell, Tarzan leaped forward and seized one of the hairy arms; and once more the body of Mal-gash flew over the head of the ape-man to crash heavily to the hard ground.

This time Mal-gash lay still; and Tarzan leaped upon him, his great hunting knife flashing in the air. "Kagoda?" he demanded.

Mal-gash, surprised, and dazed, saw the knife flashing above him, felt the fingers at his throat. "Kagoda," he said, which means either "Do you surrender?" or "I do surrender," depending upon inflection.

Tarzan rose to his feet and beat his chest, for he knew these anthropoids and he knew that a king must not only prove his right to rule but constantly impress the simple minds of his followers by chest-beating and boasting, much as a simple Fascist mind is impressed. "I am Tarzan, king of all the apes," he cried; and then he looked about the congregated apes to see if there was any who dared to question his right to rule; but they had seen what he had done to the mighty Mal-gash, and the servants of God started to drift slowly away with self-conscious nonchalance; but Tarzan called them back.

"Mal-gash is still your king," he said, "and Ungo the king of his tribe; but you will live together in peace while Ungo remains in your country. Together you will fight your common enemies; and when I, Tarzan of the Apes, call, you will come."

Mal-gash, a little shaky, clambered to his feet. "I am Mal-gash," he said, beating his breast; "I am Mal-gash, king of the apes of Ho-den."

So Mal-gash remained king of the apes of the forest; but a couple of young and powerful bulls cast speculative eyes upon him. If the puny Tarmangani could make Mal-gash say "kagoda," each of these thought he might do the same and become king; but when they appraised the great muscles and the powerful yellow fangs of Mal-gash, each decided to wait a bit.

Tarzan ranged with the apes the remainder of the day, but when night came he left them and lay up in a tree near the wall of the castle of Alemtejo.

NINETEEN . . The Mad Buffalo

As DAWN BROKE, Tarzan arose and stretched; then he sought the little stream that ran close to the wall at one end of the castle on the way to its terrific plunge over the cliff at the end of the plateau. After drinking and bathing, he sought what food the forest afforded. His plans were made, but he was in no hurry; and it was mid-morning before he approached the gates of Alemtejo.

The sentry in the barbican saw him and thought that God was returning; and the warriors who swung the gate open thought he was God, too, until after he had passed them; and then their suspicions were aroused; but before they could stop him or question him, their attention was diverted by screams and shouts from the far end of the ballium. All eyes turned in the direction of the disturbance to see frightened peasants scampering panic-stricken from the path of a snorting bull buffalo.

In the center of the ballium, directly in the path of the beast, stood a magnificent figure helmeted and cuirassed in solid gold. It was Osorio da Serra, the great noble of Alemtejo. For a moment the man hesitated, half drawing his great sword; but evidently realizing the futility of such a defense he turned and fled; and now the red-eyed beast, foam flecking its neck and sides, centered its charge upon the fleeing man, the natural reaction of any maddened animal.

As da Serra passed close to Tarzan, the ape-man saw that in another few yards the bull would overhaul its quarry. It would toss him and then it would gore and trample him.

Tarzan knew that if he stood still the animal would pass him by, its whole attention being riveted upon the man who ran, the moving figure beckoning it to pursuit.

As the bull came abreast of him, the ape-man took a few running steps close to its shoulder; then he launched himself at its head, grasping one horn and its nose, twisting the head

96

downward and to one side. The bull stumbled and went down, almost tearing loose from the ape-man's grasp; but that grip of steel still held, and though the great brute struggled, snorting and bellowing, the man twisted its head and held it so that it could not arise.

Da Serra, realizing that he could not outdistance the charging bull, had turned with drawn sword to face the oncoming beast; and so he had witnessed the act of the stranger, marveling at his courage and his superhuman strength. Now he ran toward the struggling man and beast, summoning warriors to his assistance; but before they reached the two the mighty bull wrenched his head free and staggered to his feet.

Tarzan had retained his hold upon one horn, and now he seized the other as man and beast stood facing one another. The bull shook its lowered head as, snorting and bellowing, it pawed the earth; then it surged forward to gore and trample the ape-man. The muscles of the Lord of the Jungle tensed beneath his bronzed skin, as, exerting his mighty strength, he held the bull and slowly twisted its head.

The awe-struck Alemtejos watched in wide-eyed wonder as once again the giant white man brought the great bull to its knees and then, with a final twist, rolled it over on its side.

This time Tarzan held the struggling brute until, finally, it lay still, panting and subdued; then herders came, twenty of them, and put ropes around its horns; and when Tarzan released his hold, and the buffalo scrambled to its feet, they led it away, ten men on either side.

Osorio da Serra came close to the ape-man. "I owe you my life," he said. "Who are you and how may I repay you?"

"I am Tarzan of the Apes," replied the Lord of the Jungle.

Da Serra looked his surprise. "But that cannot be," he said. "I know Tarzan of the Apes well; for two years he has been God in Alemtejo."

"I am Tarzan of the Apes," repeated the ape-man. "The other is an impostor."

The eyes of Osorio da Serra narrowed fleetingly in thought. "Come with me," he said. "You are my guest in Alemtejo."

"And who are you?" demanded Tarzan.

"I am Osorio da Serra, Captain-General of the warriors of Alemtejo."

Da Serra turned to the soldiers who were crowding close in admiration of the white giant who could throw and subdue a bull buffalo. "This, my children, is the real God," he said. "The other was an impostor"; and all within earshot dropped to their knees and crossed themselves.

By no slightest change in expression did Tarzan reveal his surprise. He would wait until he should have discovered just what this silly assumption meant to him. Perhaps it would improve his position among a strange people. He wondered what motive the man da Serra had in proclaiming him a god. He would wait and see.

"Come," said da Serra, "we will go to my apartment," and led the way into the castle.

Within the gloomy corridors, where it was not easy to distinguish features, all whom Tarzan passed knelt and crossed themselves; and word spread quickly through the castle that God had returned. It came to the ears of da Gama, who immediately summoned Ruiz the high priest.

"What is this I hear?" demanded the king—"that God has returned."

"I just heard it myself," replied Ruiz. "They say that he subdued a mad buffalo in the ballium, and that da Serra has taken him to his apartment."

"Summon them both," commanded da Gama.

In the quarters of the Captain-General of Alemtejo, da Serra was speaking earnestly to Tarzan. "You saved my life. Now let me save you from slavery or death."

"What do you mean?" asked the ape-man.

"All strangers who fall into the hands of da Gama, the king, are doomed to slavery for the remainder of their lives, or are sacrificed upon the altar of Ruiz the high priest. I mean that if we can convince the people that you are the true God, neither da Gama nor Ruiz will dare enslave or kill you. Do as I say, and you need not be afraid."

"I am not afraid," said the ape-man. "Had I been afraid, I should not have come here."

"Why did you come?" inquired da Serra.

"To kill the man who calls himself Tarzan of the Apes, and who stole women and children, bringing the hatred of my friends upon me."

"So you came here to kill God?" said da Serra. "You are a brave man to tell me that. Suppose I had believed in the man whom da Gama calls God?"

"You didn't believe in him?" asked Tarzan.

"No, neither did da Gama nor Ruiz; but the people believed

that he was God. Da Gama and Ruiz will know you are not God; but that will make no difference, if the people believe; and when they hear the story of the buffalo, they will know that no mortal man could have done the thing you did."

"But why should I deceive the people?" asked Tarzan.

"You will not be deceiving them. They will deceive themselves."

"To what purpose?" demanded the ape-man.

"Because it is easy to control the common people through their superstitions," explained da Serra. "It is for their own good; and, furthermore, it pleases them to have a god. He tells them what to do, and they believe him."

"I do not like it. I shall not say that I am God; and after I have killed the man who calls himself Tarzan, I shall go away again. Where is he? And where is the girl he brought here with him?"

"They were stolen yesterday by the Moslems during a great battle."

"You mean the negroes who attacked the castle yesterday?" asked Tarzan.

"Yes."

"They looked like Gallas to me," said the ape-man.

"They are Gallas; but they are also Moslems. Their village lies in the foothills above the plain."

"I shall go there and find him," said Tarzan.

"You would be killed," said da Serra. "The Moslems are very fierce people."

"Nevertheless, I shall go."

"There is no hurry," said da Serra. "If they have not already killed him, he will remain there a slave as long as he lives. Therefore, you can stay in Alemtejo for a while and help me."

"How can I help you?"

"Da Gama is a bad king, and Ruiz the high priest is another scoundrel. We want to get rid of them and choose a new king and a new high priest. After we find that the people have sufficient faith in you, it will only be necessary for you to command them to rise against da Gama."

"And then you will be king," suggested Tarzan.

Da Serra flushed. "Whomever the nobles and the warriors choose will be king," he said.

As da Serra ceased speaking, a messenger appeared and summoned them to the throne room by order of the king.

TWENTY . . The Sultan

HOWLING BLACKS GREETED THE PRISONERS as their escort marched them into the village of Ali, the sultan.

"Escape!" said Sandra Pickerall, bitterly. "We were infinitely better off in Alemtejo."

The man walked with bowed head. "All that I do is wrong," he said. "I have brought all this misery upon you—I who would die for you."

She touched his arm gently. "Do not reproach yourself," she said. "I know now that you did not know what you were doing; but perhaps, after all, it was fate," she added, enigmatically.

The village was a hodge-podge of grass huts, houses of sod or clay, and several constructed of native rocks. The largest of these stood in the center of the village at one side of a large plaza. To this building they were conducted, surrounded by a horde of screaming blacks. They were halted there; and presently a huge negro emerged from the interior with warriors marching on either side and before and behind him, a slave carrying an unbrella above his head, while another brushed flies from him with a bunch of feathers fastened to the end of a stick. The fat man was the sultan, Ali. He seated himself upon a stool, and his court gathered about and behind him.

The leader of the escort guarding the prisoners advanced and knelt before the sultan. "We have been victorious in our battle with the Alemtejos," he reported, "and we bring these two prisoners to our sultan."

"You dare to disturb me," cried Ali, "to bring me two of the Alemtejos' white slaves? Take them to the prison compound; and as for you—"

"Patience, O Sultan," cried the warrior. "These are no slaves. They are the god and goddess of Alemtejo."

The sultan Ali scowled. "They are not gods," he bellowed.

"There is no god but Allah. Take the man to the compound. The woman pleases me. Perhaps I shall keep her; or if the Alemtejos wish their gods returned to them, I will send them back when they send me two hundred buffaloes. Take that word to King Cristoforo—two hundred buffaloes before the full moon."

"Yes, O Sultan," cried the warrior, prostrating himself. "I go at once to Alemtejo, carrying a flag of truce."

Sandra took a step toward the black sultan. "Why would you keep us here as prisoners?" she asked in faltering Swahili. "We are not enemies. We have not harmed you. We were prisoners of the Alemtejos. Now that you have rescued us from them, let us go. We are no good to you."

"The man is strong," said Ali. "He will work in the mines. You are beautiful; but if Cristoforo sends two hundred buffaloes, I shall send you back to him."

"My father will give you more than the value of two hundred buffaloes, if you will let me go," said Sandra.

"What will he give me?" demanded Ali.

"He will give you gold," she said.

The sultan laughed. "Gold!" he exclaimed. "I have more gold than I know what to do with."

"My people are rich and powerful," insisted the girl. "There are many of them. Some day they will come and punish you, if you do not let us go."

The sultan sneered. "We do not fear the white man. They fear us. When they come, we make slaves of them. Have they ever sent soldiers against us? No; they are afraid; but enough of this. Take the man to the compound and turn the girl over to the women. Tell them to see that she is not harmed, or they will feel the wrath of Ali."

Sandra turned to the man who thought that he was Tarzan. "I guess it is quite useless," she said hopelessly.

"I am afraid so," he said; "but don't give up hope. We may find a way to escape. I shall think of nothing else."

Some women came then and took Sandra away, and a couple of warriors pushed her fellow prisoner in the opposite direction; and as he was being taken away toward the compound he kept looking back, feasting his eyes for perhaps the last time upon this girl whom he had learned to love.

The compound, a filthy place surrounded by a high palisade, was deserted. There was a single entrance closed by a heavy gate, secured upon the outside by huge bars. Inside, the man saw a shed at one end of the enclosure. Its floor was littered with dried grasses and filthy sleeping mats, while scattered about were a number of equally filthy cooking pots.

With his eyes the man gauged the height of the palisade, and as he did so he saw a human head hanging near the top. It was covered with buzzing flies, which crawled in and out of the ears, the nostrils, and the open mouth. The man turned away with a shudder of digust.

The late afternoon sun cast a shadow of one wall halfway across the compound. The man went and sat down in the shade, leaning against the wall. Physically he was not tired, but mentally he was exhausted. He continually reproached himself for the hideous wrongs he had done the girl. Through his mind ran a procession of mad schemes for her deliverance. He kept repeating to himself, "I am Tarzan. I am Tarzan. There is nothing that I cannot do;" but always he must return and face the fact that he was utterly helpless.

Late in the afternoon, the compound gates swung open and fifteen or twenty slaves filed in. All but one were emaciated and filthy blacks or Alemtejos. That one was a white man. It was Pelham Dutton.

The man leaped to his feet and hurried forward. "Dutton!" he exclaimed. "How in the world did you get here?"

The American's eyes flashed angrily. "I wish to God I had something with which to kill you," he said.

The man shook his head. "I don't blame you any," he said. "I deserve to die for what I have done; but I want to live so I can help to save her."

The American sneered. "What kind of a line is that you're handing me?" he demanded. "You stole her not once but twice. You dragged her to this infernal country. God knows what you have done to her; and now you try to tell me you want to live to save her. Do you expect me to believe that?"

The other shook his head. "No," he admitted, "I suppose not; but the fact remains that I regret what I have done and would like to help her."

"Why this sudden change of heart?" demanded Dutton, skeptically.

"You see, I never knew why I did things." Dutton noted a pained, bewildered expression in the man's eyes. "I just did everything that da Gama told me to do. I thought I had to.

I can't explain why. I don't understand it. He told me to go
and get a white woman to be a goddess; and it just happened
that Sandra Pickerall was the first white woman I found;
but after we got back to Alemtejo, I discovered that neither
the king nor the high priest believed me to be a god. They
were just using me to fool the common people. She taught
me that. She taught me a lot of things that I evidently didn't
have brains enough to discover for myself. You see, I had
always thought I was really doing her a favor by bringing her
to Alemtejo to be a goddess; but when I found that even the
man who had sent me for her did not believe she was a goddess,
when I found out how I had been deceived and made a fool
of, and made to commit this wrong, I determined then to
find some way to rescue her and take her back to her
father. We succeeded in escaping from the castle this morning and were on our way out of the country when we were
captured by these Moslems."

"Sandra was captured with you?" demanded Dutton. "She
is in the hands of these black devils?"

"Yes."

"You were really trying to take her out?" asked Dutton.

"I give you my word," said the other.

"I don't know why I should," said Dutton, "but somehow
I believe you."

"Then we can work together to get her out of here," said
the man, extending his hand as though to seal the bargain.

Dutton hesitated; then he grasped the proffered hand.

"I hope you're on the level," he said, "and somehow I feel
you are, notwithstanding your phony name and all the rest
of it."

"I thought that was my name until she told me it was not."

"Well, what is your name?" asked Dutton.

"That is the only name I know."

"Batty," thought Dutton.

"Where did you just come from?" asked the man who called
himself Tarzan.

"From the gold mine," replied Dutton. "They take us there
to work nearly every day."

"Then if they take us out of the compound, we may get
a chance to escape."

"Not on your life! They send too many warriors with us."

"We must make an opportunity then," said the man, "if
we are going to get her away from here before it is too late.

Ali has already sent a messenger to da Gama, offering to release us on payment of two hundred buffaloes; and if da Gama doesn't send the buffaloes, Ali says he will keep Sandra for himself; and you know what that means."

"Do you know where she is?" asked Dutton.

"Yes. I saw some women take her into a hut near the sultan's——palace, I suppose he calls it."

Until they sank into exhausted sleep that night, the two men schemed futilely to escape.

TWENTY-ONE . . The New God

WHEN THE KING'S MESSENGER entered the apartment of da Serra and his eyes fell upon Tarzan his demeanor expressed his amazement; and, for an instant, he half knelt. He had been sent to summon da Serra and "the stranger," and at the first glance he had thought the man was God.

In the instant that he hesitated before delivering his message, da Serra spoke sharply to him. "Kneel!" he commanded. "How dare you stand in the presence of God?"

Bewildered, the fellow dropped to one knee and crossed himself; and in that position he delivered the message from da Gama.

"Tell the king," said da Serra, "to summon the nobles and the warriors to the throne room to receive fittingly the true God who has come at last to Alemtejo"; so another convert went out through the castle to spread the word that the true God has come to Alemtejo, and the word spread like wildfire through the castle and out into the village where the common people live.

By the time the message reached the king everyone in the castle had heard it, so that the nobles and warriors commenced arriving in the throne room almost upon the heels of the messenger. There they repeated to one another with embellishments the story of the superhuman strength of this true God who could overcome a bull buffalo with his bare hands.

Da Gama was furious. "This is a trick of da Serra's," he complained to Ruiz. "He wants a God whom he can control. Listen to the fools—they have not even seen the stranger; yet already they are speaking of him as the true God. They will believe anything."

"Then why not tell them that the fellow is an impostor," counselled the high priest.

"You should tell them," countered the king. "You are high priest; so you should know God when you see him, better than any other."

Ruiz thought this over. If he denied this God and the people accepted him, he would be discredited. On the other hand, if the people accepted him, da Serra would be all-powerful, and that, Ruiz feared, might be the end of both him and da Gama. Reasoning thus, he quickly reached a decision, and stepping down from the dais he took his place behind the altar and commanded silence.

"You all know that the true God was stolen by the Moslems," he said. "If this, perchance, is the true God returned, we should all be thankful; but if it is not he, then the fellow is an impostor and should go either into slavery or to the guardians of Alemtejo."

There were murmurings in the crowded throne room; but whether in acquiescence or dissent, one could not tell.

Presently a voice rang out from the rear of the chamber. It was Osorio da Serra's. "The true God is here!" cried the Captain-General.

Every eye turned in the direction of the two men standing in the doorway, and as they advanced slowly toward the dais many knelt and crossed themselves, but many did not. "The true God," cried some. "Imposter!" cried others.

Da Serra halted in the center of the room. "Many of you have heard of how this true God stopped the charge of a maddened bull buffalo in the ballium and held him and threw him to the ground. Could the other have done this? Could any mortal man have done it? If you are still in doubt, let me ask you if you think a true God could have been captured by Moslems. He would have struck them dead."

At this, there were many cries of assent, and more warriors and nobles dropped to their knees. Some of the nobles turned to Ruiz. "Is this man the true God?" they demanded.

"No," shouted the high priest. "He is an imposter."

"This is a trick of da Serra's," cried da Gamma. "Seize them both, the impostor and the traitor. To the lions with them!"

A few nobles and warriors rushed toward Tarzan and da Serra.

"Down with da Gama and Ruiz," shouted the latter, drawing his sword.

A warrior struck at Tarzan with his heavy broadsword, but the ape-man leaped to one side and, closing with his antagonist, lifted him high above his head and hurled him heavily in the faces of his fellows. After that there was a lull, and a voice cried out, "Down with da Gama. Long live King Osorio"; and, like magic, nobles and warriors clustered

around da Serra and Tarzan, offering a ring of steel blades
to the handful who had remained loyal to da Gama.

Ruiz the high priest cursed and reviled, exhorting the
warriors to remain faithful to their king and to the true God,
who, he promised, would soon return to them; but he who
had been so feared was equally hated. Hands reached
for him, and he fled screaming through the small doorway
at the back of the dais; and with him went King Cristoforo. Thus did Osorio da Serra become king of Alemtejo, and
Tarzan of the Apes the true God.

As da Serra and Tarzan took their places on the thrones
upon the dais, the priest Quesada emerged from the crowd and
knelt before the ape-man.

Da Serra leaned toward Tarzan. "This is your new high
priest," he whispered. "Announce him to the people."

Now Tarzan did not like the part he was playing nor did
he know how a god should act; so he said nothing, and it was
finally da Serra who ordained Quesada high priest of Alemtejo.

The new king ordered a feast for all; and while it was
being prepared, word was brought him that a detachment of
warriors had returned with three white slaves and five loads
of salt and iron.

Da Serra ordered them brought to the throne room.
"It is a good omen," he said, "at the beginning of my reign.
We seldom capture white slaves; and not in the memory of
the oldest man have we captured three at the same time."

Tarzan was becoming bored and restless. Everything these
men did seemed silly to him. Their credulity was amazing. He
compared them with the apes, and the apes lost nothing
by the comparison. Whatever the apes did had some purpose-
ful and practical meaning. These men changed gods and
rulers without knowing whether or not they were bettering
themselves. When the apes changed kings they knew they had
a more powerful leader to direct and protect them.

Tarzan rose and stretched. He had decided that he had
had enough and that he was going away, and when he arose
everyone fell to his knees and crossed himself. The ape-man
looked at them in surprise and at that moment saw warriors
entering the throne room with three white men and recognized two of them as Crump and Minsky. Here was
something of interest. Tarzan sat down again and the nobles
and warriors rose to their feet.

As the three men were pushed forward toward the

dais, Crump voiced a profane exclamation of surprise. He nudged Minsky. "Look," he said, "the damned ape-man."

"And he's sittin' on a throne," said Minsky. "I'd hate to be in your boots. You won't never live to see no gold mine."

As the three sat at the foot of the dais, Tarzan accorded Crump and Minsky scarcely a glance; but his gaze rested on Bolton-Chilton.

"You are an Englishman?" asked Tarzan.

"Yes."

"How do you come to be in the company of these two men?"

"The men who captured me happened to capture them, later," replied Bolton-Chilton.

"Then they are not your friends?" asked the ape-man.

"I never saw them before."

"How did you happen to get captured?" asked Tarzan.

"I was captured two years ago by the Gallas of old Sultan Ali, and the other day these blighters got me."

"You lived in the Galla village for two years?"

"Yes. Why?"

"Perhaps I can use you and get you out of here into the bargain."

"Are you the chief?" asked the Englishman.

The shadow of a smile touched the ape-man's lips. "No," he said, jerking his head toward da Serra; "he is king. I am God."

Bolton-Chilton whistled. "That's rather top-hole, anyway, I should say, if a fellow doesn't take it too seriously." He had noted the smile.

"I don't," said Tarzan.

"What is he saying?" demanded da Serra. "Do you know him?"

"I know them all," said Tarzan. "This man is my friend. I will take him. The others you may do with as you please."

"Hold on now," said da Serra. "After all, I shall decide. I am king, you know."

"But I am God," said the ape-man, "or at least all those people out there think so. Do I get my man without trouble?"

Da Serra was not a bad sort, but his kingship was new to him and he was jealous of his authority. "After all," he said, "I owe you a great deal. You may have that man as your slave."

When Crump and Minsky were taken away to the slave

quarters, Chilton was left behind; and at the conclusion of the feast he accompanied Tarzan and da Serra back to the latter's apartment.

Tarzan crossed to a window and looked out across the thatched village toward the distant mountains. Finally he turned to Bolton-Chilton. "You know the Galla village well?" he asked. "You know their customs and their fighting strength?"

"Yes," replied Chilton.

"There is a man there I have come a long way to kill," said the ape-man; "and a prisoner with him is an English girl whom I should like to rescue. It will be easier if I have someone with me who knows the ground thoroughly; and at the same time, if I am successful, you will be able to escape."

The other shook his head. "There is no escape," he said. "You will only be captured yourself, God or no God," he added, with a grin.

The same half-smile curved the ape-man's lips. "I know that I am not God," he said; "but I do know I am Tarzan of the Apes."

Bolton-Chilton looked at him in surprise; then he laughed. "First God, and now Tarzan of the Apes!" he exclaimed. "What next? The archbishop of Canterbury? I have never seen any of them, but any one of them is famous and powerful enough."

It was evident to Tarzan that the man did not believe him, but that was immaterial. He turned to da Serra. "The man I am going to kill, and an English girl, are prisoners in the Galla village."

"Yes," said da Serra, "I know. A messenger came this morning from the Sultan Ali, offering to release the man and the woman if da Gama would send two hundred buffaloes as a ransom. Da Gama refused."

"Let us go there and get them," said Tarzan.

"What do you mean?" asked da Serra.

"Let us take all your warriors and attack the village."

"Why should I do that?" demanded da Serra.

"You have just become king, and I notice that they didn't all accept you enthusiastically. If you immediately win a great victory over your enemies, you will command the loyalty of all your warriors. Men like kings who win battles."

"Perhaps you are right," said da Serra. "At least, it is worth thinking about."

TWENTY-TWO . . The Battle

CLOTHED IN THE GORGEOUS HABILIMENTS that da Gama had thought befitting a goddess, Sandra Pickerall lay in the squalor and filth of a Galla hut waiting almost apathetically for whatever blow Fate might next deliver her. If da Gama sent the two hundred buffaloes to ransom her and her fellow prisoner, they would at least be together again, though she felt that she would be no safer one place than the other.

Her mind dwelt much upon this man who had come into her life to alter it so completely. She no longer reproached him, because she felt he was not responsible. At first, she had thought he might be demented; but the better she had come to know him the more convinced she had become that this was not true. While she had never encountered any cases of amnesia, she knew enough about it from hearsay and from reading to convince her that the man was a victim of this strange affliction. The mystery surrounding him piqued her curiosity. Who was he? What had he been? She thought about him so continually that she began to be a little frightened as she questioned herself; but she was honest and she had to admit that from hate had grown friendship that was verging upon an attachment even stronger.

She caught her breath at the realization. How terrible it would be to permit herself to fall in love with a man concerning whom she knew absolutely nothing—a man who knew absolutely nothing about himself. He might be a criminal, or, even worse, he might be married.

No, she must not think such thoughts. She must put him out of her mind entirely; but that was easier thought than done. Regardless of her good intentions, he kept obtruding himself upon her every revery; and, laboring in the gold mine beneath the hot, African sun, the man, on the contrary, strove to conjure memories of the girl and revel in the knowledge that he loved her; notwithstanding the fact that he realized

110

the hopelessness of his infatuation; and Dutton, working beside him, fed upon similar memories and was gladdened by his love of the same girl. It was well for the peace of mind of each that he could not read the thoughts of the other.

While the Galla overseers were hard taskmasters, they were not unnecessarily cruel. Though several of them carried whips, they seldom used them, and then only to spur on an obvious shirker; but if the men were not cruel to their charges, the older women would have treated Sandra with every indignity and cruelty had they not feared Ali, who had given orders that she was not to be harmed.

There was a young girl who brought her food who was kind to her, and from her she learned that the messenger had returned from da Gama and that the king of Alemtejo had refused to ransom her and the man who thought he was Tarzan.

She asked the girl what was to become of her; and the answer was not long in coming, as an old hag entered the hut snarling through yellow fangs, cursing and raging as she spread what was now common gossip in the village. Ali had proclaimed the white prisoner his new wife and had set the day for the marriage rites.

The old hag was furious, because as the oldest wife of the sultan it was her duty to supervise the preparation of the bride.

Sandra was frantic. She pleaded with the young girl who had been kind to her to bring her a knife that she might destroy herself; but the girl was afraid. The marriage was to be celebrated with a feast and orgy of drinking the following day and consummated at night; in the meantime she must find some way to escape or kill herself; but she was being so closely watched now that the accomplishment of either seemed impossible.

After the slaves returned from the mine the gossip filtered into the prisoners' compound. The two white men heard it and were appalled.

"We must get out of here," said the man who thought he was Tarzan.

Dutton pointed to the grisly head swinging from the top of the palisade. "That is what happens to slaves who try to escape," he said.

"Nevertheless, we must try," insisted the other. "Perhaps tomorrow, marching to or from the mine, we may find an opportunity;" but the next day brought no opportunity as they trod the familiar path to the mine.

In the village, preparations for the celebration were under way. Food and beer were being prepared; and the terrified bride was being instructed as to her part in the rites.

In mid-afternoon a warrior, breathless from exertion, entered the village and ran to the sultan's palace, where he reported to Ali that he had seen an army of Alemtejos encamped in the hills behind the village.

This was a new technique, and it bewildered Ali. Always before, the Alemtejos had come charging across the plain with blaring trumpets and hoarse war-cries. To have them sneak upon him thus from the rear was something new. He wondered why they had gone into camp. That seemed a strange thing to do if they had come to make war. One of his head men suggested they might be waiting to attack after dark; and Ali was scandalized. Such a thing had never been done before.

The sultan gave orders to recall the soldiers and slaves from the mine and to arm all the slaves, for the report he had received led him to believe that the Alemtejos might far out-number his own fighting men.

Notwithstanding the preparations for battle, the preparations for the wedding went on as contemplated.

In all that went on, Sandra had no part, being kept under close guard in her hut; but the bridegroom ate and drank much beer, as did his warriors; and what with the dancing and feasting and drinking, the enemy at their gate was almost forgotten.

Scarcely a mile away, hidden in the hills, a thousand buffaloes were being herded slowly toward the village as night was falling. The chariots of war had been left behind in Alemtejo, for this was to the Alemtejos a new style of war and they accepted it because it had been ordered by their God.

On one flank of the slowly marching buffaloes marched Tarzan and Chilton; and behind the Lord of the Jungle came Ungo and Mal-gash with all their apes. Tarzan knew that herding these half-domesticated buffaloes at night was fraught with danger. As darkness fell, they had become more and more nervous and irritable; but they were still moving slowly toward the village, and they were, much to his relief, remarkably quiet. What little lowing and bellowing there was was drowned out in the village by the shouts and yells of the dancers and the screams of the women.

Sultan Ali, half drunk and reeling, entered the hut where Sandra Pickerall was confined. Pushing the women aside, he seized the girl by the arm and dragged her out of the hut and toward his palace, just as a sentry rushed into the village shouting a warning.

"The Alemtejos come!" he screamed. "The Alemtejos are here!"

The shock seemed to sober Ali. He dropped Sandra's arm and commenced to shout orders rapidly to his headmen and his warriors. The armed slaves were released from the compound and were herded into line at the edge of the village facing the oncoming Alemtejos.

"Now is our chance," the man who thought he was Tarzan whispered to Dutton. "Work your way slowly over this way with me, toward Sandra's hut. During the confusion of the fighting, we'll get her out of here."

Out in the night beyond the village, Tarzan issued the command for which the warriors of Alemtejo had been waiting; and at that signal, trumpets blared as war-cries rang out behind the startled buffaloes. Warriors rushed at the rear guard of the shaggy beasts, belaboring them with the hafts of spears. Bellowing and snorting, the frightened beasts broke into a run; and presently the whole great herd was charging toward the village of Ali the Sultan; and with them raced Tarzan and Chilton and the band of great apes.

Confusion and chaos reigned in the village, as the thundering beasts came charging through. The false Tarzan ran to Sandra's hut and called her, but there was no response. The girl was standing where Ali had left her in the shadow of the palace.

Some of the Gallas stood their ground, hurling spears and firebrands at the charging buffaloes. Others turned and fled with the women and children from the path of the now maddened beasts, only to be set upon by the apes of Ungo and Mal-gash.

Sandra Pickerall heard the Alemtejo warriors shouting behind the herd of buffalo and realized that in a few minutes they would enter the village and she would be re-captured. She saw an opening in the herd as it scattered out; and she darted through it, hoping to escape from the village. The false Tarzan saw her and ran toward her, followed by Dutton.

He called her by name and, seizing her hand, ran dodging among the buffaloes, until presently they were clear of the herd and out of the village. Shielded by the darkness, they hurried on, with the bellowing of the buffaloes, the roaring of the apes, and the shouts of the warriors still ringing in their ears but in diminishing volume as they increased their distance from the village.

Once Sandra glanced back. "Someone is following us," she said.

"That's Dutton," said the man.

Sandra stopped and turned about. "Pelham!" she cried. "Is it really you?"

The happiness in her voice fell like cold lead on the heart of the man who thought he was Tarzan, for he guessed that Dutton loved the girl and realized there was every reason why Sandra should return his love; whereas, as far as he was concerned, he deserved nothing but her loathing and contempt.

Dutton ran forward with outstretched hands. "Oh, Sandra," he cried, "what you have gone through! But maybe it is over now. Maybe we can get out of this accursed country, after all."

As they moved on through the night, Sandra and Dutton recounted to each other the adventures they had passed through since they had been separated. They seemed very happy, but the man walking a little behind them was sad.

TWENTY-THREE . . In Hiding

THE ROUT OF THE GALLAS was complete; and as the buffaloes finally passed on out of the village, Osorio da Serra and his warriors entered it. They found Tarzan searching for the girl and for the man he had come to kill; but the search was futile; and Tarzan surmised that they had escaped from the village with the fugitive blacks. It was useless to look for them tonight. Tomorrow he would find them. But they did find Sultan Ali hiding in his palace; and Osorio da Serra took him prisoner to carry back to Alemtejo in triumph.

The victorious Alemtejos made themselves at home in the village, finishing the feast and the beer that the Gallas had left behind.

Tarzan called the apes; and as they gathered about him, he told them to go back to their own countries, for he realized that not even he could hold them much longer; and presently they wandered out of the village, much to the relief of the Alemtejo warriors.

"And now what?" asked Chilton. "It looks to me like a good time for me to make my getaway."

Tarzan nodded. "We'll both go presently," he said. "I want to take one more look around the village to make sure that the man I came to kill is not here."

"Do you really mean that you came into this country just to find this man and kill him?" asked Chilton. "Why, you can't do that, you know. That would be murder."

"If you crushed a poisonous spider with your boot, you wouldn't call that murder," replied the ape-man. "To me, this man is no better than a spider."

"He must have done something pretty awful to you," ventured Bolton-Chilton.

"He did. He stole my name, and then took the women and children of my friends and carried them away to slavery or death."

"What did he call himself?" asked the Englishman.

"Tarzan of the Apes."

115

Bolton-Chilton scratched his head. "It must be contagious," he said.

Tarzan went through the village again, searching the huts and questioning the Alemtejo warriors and their prisoners; but he found no trace either of Sandra or the man he sought; and presently he came back to Chilton, and the two left the village without attracting attention.

"Do you know," said Chilton, "I always thought all those native villages were surrounded by a palisade."

"The situation here is unique," replied Tarzan. "Da Serra explained it to me. The Gallas have only one enemy——the Alemtejos; and for four hundred years the latter's method of attack has always been the same. They come across the plain with blaring trumpets and war-cries. The Gallas rush out and meet them. There is a very brief conflict in which some men are killed and some taken prisoners; then each side returns to its village. The Alemtejos have never before attempted to enter the village of the Gallas. The idea this time was mine, because, otherwise, I could not have found the girl nor the man for whom I sought."

"The Gallas had better start building a palisade," said Chilton.

They walked on in silence for a time, and then the Englishman asked Tarzan what his plans were.

"I shall find my man; and after I have killed him, I'll take you down to some settlement on the Congo where you can get transportation out of the country."

"I understand there are only two trails out of here," said Bolton-Chilton.

"I know of only one," replied Tarzan, "and it's a rather nasty descent over a cliff."

"I have heard of that," said the other; "but I have twice been over an easy trail, which I think I can find again, and we won't have to go anywhere near Alemtejo and risk recapture."

"All right," replied the ape-man, "we will find the other trail."

"But how about the girl?"

"He probably has her with him," said Tarzan.

*   *   *

While da Serra had been preparing to march out of Alemtejo with his army, all of the slaves had been detailed to round up the buffaloes that were to be driven ahead of the advancing force; and in the confusion, Crump and Minsky had succeeded in escaping into the woods behind the castle, where they hid until night fell; then, after night had fallen, they started out across the plain towards the mountains.

"In the morning," said Crump, "we'll look around for that gold mine."

"In the morning," retorted Minsky, "we'll look for the trail out of this damned country! I don't want no part of it, gold mine or no gold mine."

"If I'd knowed you was yellow," said Crump, "I wouldn't have brought you along."

"If I'd knowed you didn't have no more sense than a jackass, I wouldn't have come," retorted Minsky. "What with havin' no weapons to kill game with or nothin', I should be wastin' my time lookin' for a gold mine. Outside of lookin' for the trail that'll take me out of here, the only other thing I got time to look for is food."

Crump grumbled as he plodded along. He didn't like the idea of being alone, even though his companion was as helpless as he; but the lure of the gold was stronger than any other force that played within him.

Because they had taken a circuitous route in order to avoid meeting any of the Alemtejo warriors who might be returning from the Galla village, it was almost morning when, hungry, dirty, and exhausted, the two men reached the hills and lay down to rest. In the same hills Sandra, Dutton, and the man who thought he was Tarzan also were hiding.

Sandra was the first to awaken in the morning. She saw the men stretched on either side of her protectively. She had slept but fitfully and was far from rested; so she did not disturb them, being content to lie there quietly. Through her mind ran the strange sequence of events that had been crowded into the past long weeks of danger and hopelessness which made it seem an eternity since she had been snatched from the protection of her father. She was free. She tried to think only of that, as she dared not look into the future that offered little more of hope than had the past.

She was free, but for how long? If she were not recaptured by the Gallas or the Alemtejos, she still had the horrid Waruturi country to pass through; and there was always the menace of predatory beasts as well as predatory men, her only protection these two men armed with the bows, arrows and spears which had been given them at the order of Ali the

Sultan when he had commanded that the slaves be placed in the front rank to meet the attacking Alemtejos. What protection could these pitiful weapons offer against Waruturi, lion, or leopard? She knew these two to be brave men, but they were not super-men; and then she thought of Tarzan of the Apes whom she believed Crump had killed. How safe she had felt with him!

Her head turned and her eyes rested upon the man who had stolen Tarzan's name, and at once her mind was filled with speculation as to who and what he really was. She watched his chest rise and fall to his regular breathing. She saw a lock of tousled hair falling across his forehead, and she wanted to reach out and brush it back. It was an urge to caress, and she realized it and was puzzled and ashamed. She turned her head then and looked at Dutton. Here was a man of her own caste, a man whom she was confident loved her; yet she felt no urge to brush his forehead with her palm. The girl sighed and closed her eyes. Here was something more to plague and harrass her, as though the other trials which confronted her were not enough. She wished she had never seen the man who called himself Tarzan; but when next she opened her eyes they looked straight into his. He smiled, and the world took on a new effulgence and she was glad that she was alive and here, for he was here. A realization of her reaction brought a sudden flush to her face, but she smiled back and said, "Good morning."

Dutton awoke then and sat up. "We ought to be making our plans," he said. "We had no opportunity last night. Personally, I think we ought to hide here in the hills for several days; and then, at night, make our way past Alemtejo to the cliff."

Sandra shuddered. "I know I can never go down there," she said.

"There is another way out," said the man who thought he was Tarzan. "They say it is a very much easier way, but I do not know where it is. I think it is somewhere in this direction;" and he pointed toward the northwest.

"While we are waiting here in the hills then," suggested Sandra, "let's look for it. If there is another way out, there should be a trail leading to it."

"We've got to find food," said Dutton; "so let's look for it in that direction;" and so the three set forth toward the northwest.

TWENTY-FOUR .. Captured by Great Apes

THE APES OF UNGO and the apes of Mal-gash had wandered off
into the hills after the battle, the two bands separating almost
immediately; and in the morning each band started out in
search of food.

Naturally nervous, suspicious, and short-tempered, the great
beasts were doubly dangerous now, for they were not only
hungry but were still emotionally unstrung as a result of the
battle of the previous night.

They were constantly quarrelling among themselves; and
had the two bands remained together there would have been a
pitched battle eventually, for between different tribes of apes
there is no more feeling of brotherhood than there is between
different tribes of men. They do not search each other out
solely for the purpose of killing one another, as men do; but
an accidental meeting may easily result in bloodshed.

Sandra Pickerall and her two companions were also searching for food, but so far without any success. The girl was very
tired. She wondered how much longer she could go on, mar-
velling at the punishment that human flesh could endure; but
she made no complaint. Dutton was the weaker of the two
men, for he had been longer on the poor fare of a Galla slave,
nor had he the splendid physique of the man who said he was
Tarzan; but neither did he by sign or word give evidence that
he felt he was nearing exhaustion.

However, the other man noted the occasional faltering steps
of his companions. "You are both very tired," he said. "Perhaps it would be better if you stopped here and rested while I
hunt for food. There is a patch of bamboo ahead of us and to
the left a forest. In one or the other, I may find game."

"I do not think we should separate," said Sandra. "There is
always strength in numbers, even though they are few; and at
least there is a feeling of greater security."

"I quite agree," said Dutton. "Let's stick together until one
of us can go no farther; then we can decide what to do. In the

119

meantime, we may bag game; and a good meal will certainly give us renewed strength."

The other man nodded his assent. "Just as you say," he agreed. "At least, we should find a safer and more concealed spot than this."

As they talked, close-set, angry eyes watched them from the concealment of the bamboo thicket toward which they were moving; and when the three had come very close to it, the owner of the eyes turned to move away. "There's something in there," said the man who called himself Tarzan, "some big animal. I am going to take a chance." And with that, he swiftly fitted an arrow to his bow and shot the missile into the thicket at the form he could dimly see moving there.

Instantly there was a scream of pain and rage, a crashing of bamboo, and a huge bull ape burst into view; then the whole thicket seemed to burst into life. It swayed and groaned and crashed to the great bodies of a dozen more apes responding to the cry of their fellow.

Sandra was appalled as the great beasts lumbered forward toward them, growling and beating their mighty chests. "The servants of God!" exclaimed the man who called himself Tarzan; and then he spoke to them in the language the Alemtejos had taught them. He commanded them to stop; and for a moment they hesitated, but only for a moment; and then, led by the wounded bull, they charged.

The two men had time to discharge a single arrow each; but these only served to infuriate the apes the more. Perhaps they recognized the man who had been God, the man who called himself Tarzan; but if they did, their former allegiance to him was dissipated by the rage engendered by his attack upon them.

The two men dropped their bows and picked up their spears, standing ready to defend themselves and Sandra with their lives. The girl might have run then and possibly made her escape; but instead, she stood behind her men, waiting and watching. How puny and helpless they looked beside these hairy monsters and how superlatively courageous.

She saw the man who called himself Tarzan lunge at an ape with his spear, and she saw the beast seize it and tear it from the man's grasp as easily as though he had been a little child; and then she saw the ape swing the spear and crash it against the side of the man's head. Down went one of her defenders, dead, she thought; and then another huge bull seized Dutton.

The man struggled, striking futilely with his fists; but the great beast dragged him close and sank his yellow fangs in his jugular; and then it was that Sandra turned to run. There was nothing she could do to aid her companions, both of whom were quite evidently dead. Now she must think of herself; but she had taken only a few steps when a great, hairy paw fell upon her shoulder and she was dragged back with such violence that she fell to the ground.

A mighty ape stood over her, growling and roaring, and presently she was surrounded by the others. Another bull came and attempted to seize her. Her captor, roaring, leaped upon him; and as the two locked in deadly combat, a young bull picked her from the ground and, carrying her under one huge arm, lumbered away as fast as his short legs and the burden he was carrying permitted.

But he was not to get off with his prize so easily. Another bull pursued him, and presently he was obliged to drop his captive and turn upon his fellow.

Bruised, terrified, almost exhausted, Sandra with difficulty staggered to her feet. She saw the forest a short distance ahead. If she could only reach it she might find sanctuary among the trees. She glanced back. The two bulls were still fighting, and the other apes were not following her. There was a chance and she seized upon it. Momentarily endowed with new power by the emergency confronting her, she managed to run, where a few minutes before she had felt she could not for much longer even walk.

But her flight was short-lived. The bull that had run off with her had bested his antagonist, and while the latter backed away, growling, the other turned and pursued Sandra. It was only a matter of seconds before he had overhauled her. Again he picked her from the ground and waddled off toward the forest. Glancing back, Sandra saw that the other apes were now following. They were not pursuing, they were merely following; but the ape which carried her evidently did not dare stop for fear the others would overhaul him and take his prize away; and so he lumbered on into the forest followed by the entire band, while back beside the bamboo thicket lay the bodies of Pelham Dutton and the man who called himself Tarzan.

TWENTY-FIVE . . Alone

ALL DAY, Crump and Minsky had searched unavailingly for food. They had found water, and that was all that had permitted them to carry on at all. They were close to exhaustion when they lay down at dusk. The night grew cold, and they huddled together shivering. They heard a lion roar as it came down out of the hills to hunt; and they were terrified. Later, they heard him growl again, and he sounded very close. The lion had growled as he came upon the bodies of the two men. At first he was startled by the scent of man, and a little fearful; but presently he came closer and sniffed at one of the bodies. He was not a man-eater and he did not like the odor of this meat; but he was ravenously hungry and presently he seized the body by one shoulder and, lifting it, carried it deep into the bamboo thicket.

Perhaps the dead man had saved the life of Crump or Minsky, for the lion would hunt no more that night.

With the coming of dawn, the lion, his belly filled, pushed his way deeper into the thicket and lay down to sleep. Crump and Minsky, numb and stiff, staggered to their feet. "We got to keep movin'," said the latter. "We can't just lie here and either starve to death or freeze to death."

"Maybe we could find some birds' eggs or somethin' in that bamboo," suggested Crump.

"There's a forest the other side of it," said his companion. "We ought to find somethin' in one of 'em."

They moved on then in the direction of the bamboo thicket; and presently Minsky, who was ahead, stopped. "What's that?" he demanded pointing.

"It's a man," said Crump. "He's been sleepin' there. He's just gettin' up. Why, it's that ape, Tarzan!"

"No," said Minsky, "it's the other one, the guy that kept swipin' the girl."

"The girl!" said Crump. "I wonder where she is? She's still good for £3000, if we can find her."

"And get her through the Waruturi country," added Minsky.

The man who thought he was Tarzan was sitting up and looking around. He had just regained consciousness. He was cold and numb and stiff. He looked about him for Sandra and Dutton, but he saw neither of them; then he saw the two men approaching, and recognized them. What were they doing here? He knew they were bad men. He wondered if they had had anything to do with the disappearance of Sandra; then he suddenly recalled the attack of the apes. He had been badly stunned by the blow of the spear and his wits were slow in returning. He stood up and faced the two men.

"I ought to kill the guy," said Crump to Minsky in a low tone that did not reach the ears of the man awaiting their coming.

"What'd you kill him with?" demanded Minsky. "Maybe you'd scare him to death, eh? You ain't got nothin' but your mouth to kill him with."

They were coming closer to the man now. "Hello," called Crump.

The man nodded. "How did you get here?" he demanded. "Have you seen anything of Miss Pickerall?"

"No," replied Crump, "not since you stole her from my camp. What have you done with her? Where is she?"

"She and Dutton were with me until late yesterday afternoon; then we were set upon by a band of great apes, and that is the last that I remember until just now. One of them cracked me over the head with my spear. Dutton and Miss Pickerall must have been carried off by the apes."

"Maybe they weren't," suggested Minsky. "Maybe they just run out on you. You know, he was pretty soft on the girl and they didn't neither of 'em have much use for you after you stole her a couple of times."

"I don't believe they would do that," said the man. "We are good friends now, and I was trying to take her back to her father."

"Look at the blood there," said Crump. "There must have been a gallon of it. Was you wounded?"

"No," replied the man who called himself Tarzan. "It must have been one of the others." He knelt and examined the great pool of blood which was still only partly coagulated.

"Which one?" asked Minsky.

"I wish to God I knew," said the man. "It might have been either of them."

"If they killed one and took the other," said Crump, "it would have been the girl they took, not the man."

"I've got to follow them and find out," said the man who called himself Tarzan.

"We'll go with you," said Crump; "but we aint had nothin' to eat for so long that our bellies are wrapped around our backbones. You got a bow and arrow. You can do some huntin' while we're lookin'."

"Yes," said the man, "come;" and he started in the direction of the forest, following the plain spoor of the great apes.

*   *   *

When Sandra had been carried off by the bull-ape the afternoon before, the creature had been kept constantly on the move by his fellows who dogged his trail. He had dragged Sandra through brush—he had scraped her against trees and bushes. Her flesh was scratched and torn, and her golden breastplate and skirt of gold mesh had been scraped from her body in numerous occasions. However, they had held and had formed some protection from the hazards of this hideous journey.

The girl had thought that other situations in which she had found herself during the past weeks had been hopeless, but now they faded into insignificance when compared with this—alone and unarmed, a captive of great apes with the only two men who might have saved her lying dead where they had tried to defend her.

The apes of Ungo fed in the forest. It was a poor hunting ground, and they were hungry and irritable. Often they quarreled among themselves; and Ungo, the king ape, had often to chastise one of his subjects in order to keep the peace. He had just separated Zu-tho and another ape, both of whom wanted the same caterpillar, when Ga-un voiced a warning kreeg-ah!

Instantly, every member of the band became alert to danger. Listening, they heard something approaching; and presently they saw the cause of Ga-un's alarm. It was Sancho, one of the servants of God, coming toward them with a she-tarmangani beneath one hairy arm. When he first came in sight, he was looking back at the apes which were following him; and so did not immediately see the apes of Ungo. When he did, he stopped and bared his great fangs in warning. Ungo voiced a challenge and approached, followed by his great bulls. Sancho fell back, screaming his own challenges and summoning his fellows.

Ungo rushed forward and seized the girl by an arm, trying to wrest her from the grasp of Sancho. They pulled and tugged while they struck at each other with their free paws, and would have torn her apart had not the other servants of God come upon the scene, precipitating a battle that caused both Sancho and Ungo to relinquish their hold upon the girl, so they might defend themselves.

Sandra fell to the ground while the great apes fought above and around her. She saw them rend one another with their powerful fangs and strike terrific blows with their great paws, screaming and roaring in pain and rage.

It was a battle of the primordials, such as the ancestors of the first men might have waged for possession of a prize. It was bestial and primitive, lacking the civilizing refinements of machine guns and poison gas and far less effective, for the wounds were, for the most part, superficial, and the noise far more a *sine qua non* than destruction.

As they pushed and pulled, and shoved and hauled, snarling, biting, screaming, the apes of Ungo slowly pushed the servants of God back. Sandra Pickerall saw her chance then and crawled away, unnoticed. Glancing back, she saw that the apes were paying no attention to her; and so she came laboriously to her feet and staggered away into the forest.

For some time, she could hear the sound of battle diminishing in the distance; and Sandra Pickerall found herself again free, but alone in a strange forest with nothing to look forward to but death by starvation or beneath the fangs and talons of some wild beast. These things she feared, but she feared them less than she feared man.

TWENTY-SIX . . Gold

CRUMP, MINSKY, and "Tarzan" searching for signs of the girl, searching for food, found neither one nor the other. They were tired and discouraged, Crump and Minsky practically exhausted. "Tarzan" was hungry, but his mind was not on food. It was occupied with thoughts of Sandra Pickerall and conjecture as to her fate. Had it been her blood or Dutton's that they had seen on the turf near the bamboo thicket? That it was the blood of one of them, he was positive; and if one of them had been killed, how could the other have escaped? He did not concur in Crump's theory that she had been carried off by apes, for though he had often heard stories of great apes stealing women and carrying them off he had never believed them. It seemed to him more probable that some wild beast had made off with the bodies of both Dutton and Sandra; yet his love for the girl would not permit him to abandon search for her while there remained the slightest vestige of a doubt as to her fate. The result was that his hunting was perfunctory and, consequently, most unsuccessful.

Although he thought he was Tarzan, his woodcraft was little better than that of an ordinary civilized man; and so it was that he lost the trail of the great apes and followed a false trail which led farther up into the hills. That little digression was to have tragic consequences.

"This is a hell of a country," said Minsky. "I aint even seen nothin' as big as a grasshopper; and believe you me, if I seen one, I'd eat it. God, how I'd like a bowl of bouillabaisse."

"Shut up!" snapped Crump. "Another crack like that an I'll—"

"You'll do nothin'" interrupted Minsky. "And after the bouillabaisse, I'll have ham and eggs."

Crump lunged at him but missed and fell down. Minsky laughed at him. "Or maybe a great big thick steak smothered in onions!"

126

"Cut it out," said "Tarzan." "Things are bad enough as they are, without starting a fight."

"Who do you think you are to tell me what I can do and what I can't?" demanded Minsky. "If I want oysters on the half-shell, or apple pie, or crêpes suzette, I'm gonna have 'em and nobody aint gonna stop me."

"I'll stop your talking about them," said "Tarzan" slapping him with his open palm across the cheek. It was not a very hard blow, but Minsky stumbled backwards and sat down heavily. "Now listen," continued the man who said he was Tarzan, "you'll cut all this scrapping out, both of you, or I'll leave you; and without my bow and arrows, you'll never get any food."

"I aint seen you kill nothin' yet," said Crump.

"You heard me," said "Tarzan." "Take it or leave it;" then he turned and moved on up a little ravine through which the trail ran. Crump and Minsky scrambled to their feet and followed, sullen and morose, full of hatred for the man, full of hatred for one another.

Presently they came to an excavation in the side of the ravine. "Tarzan" stopped at the edge of this and looked down. The excavation was perhaps twenty-five feet deep and covered about half an acre. The path led down into it.

Crump and Minsky came and stood beside him; and at the first glance into the hole, Crump voiced a cry of elation. "The mine!" he exclaimed. "Gold! Gold! Look at it!" and then he staggered down the trail with Minsky close at his heels.

It was indeed the fabulous mine of the Alemtejos and the Gallas, temporarily abandoned because of the battle and the capture of Ali. Great lumps of pure gold that had been mined, but had not yet been removed, lay scattered over the workings.

Crump fell on them, greedily gathering together the largest he could find. "These are mine," he cried.

"What are you going to do with it?" asked "Tarzan."

"What am I going to do with it, you dope? I'm goin' to take it back to England. I'll be rich, that's what I'll be." He slipped off his coat and, laying it on the ground, commenced to pile gold into it.

Minsky was similarly engaged. "I'm gonna get me a yacht," he said, "and a French chef."

"How far do you think you can carry that stuff?" demanded "Tarzan." "You can hardly carry yourselves as it is."

"You could help us, if you had a coat," said Crump. "Wait," he added, "I'll take off my pants—they'll hold a lot."

"You can leave your pants on," said "Tarzan." "I don't intend to carry any of the stuff."

"What!" demanded Crump. "You mean you aint gonna help us? You mean you're gonna let all this stuff lie around here for a bunch of savages that don't know what to do with it? This is gold, man, gold! It will buy anything in the world—women, wine, horses. With enough of this, I could buy me a title—Sir Thomas Crump. It don't sound so bad neither."

"You're balmy," said Minsky. "They don't make lords out of the likes o'you. You gotta be a toff."

Crump ignored him and turned back on "Tarzan." "No wonder you aint got no sense enough to wear pants," he said. "Help us carry some of this out and we'll split with you. You're stronger than we are, and you could carry twice as much."

The man shook his head. "I am not interested," he said. "I am going on to hunt and look for Miss Pickerall. If you want to get out of this country alive, you'd better forget this foolishness and come along with me."

"Not on your life," said Crump. "Go on and hunt. I'll get out of this country and I'll take this gold with me."

"Tarzan" shrugged and turned back down the ravine, for seeing that the trail ended at the mine he knew he had come in the wrong direction and must go back and try to pick up the ape spoor where he had lost it.

"How much of this here stuff do you suppose we can carry?" asked Minsky. He gathered up the corners of his coat and tested the weight of his load. "Golly, but that's heavy," he said.

Crump kept piling more gold into his stack. "I'm afraid that's about all I can lug," he said finally; then he fastened the coat together as best he could and tried to lift the load to his shoulder; but he could not even raise it from the ground.

"I guess you'll have to leave the knighthood behind," said Minsky sneeringly.

"I ought to kill you," said Crump.

Minsky laughed at him, a taunting, sneering laugh; then he fastened his own coat around his hoard of gold and struggled to raise it from the ground. Finally he got it up on one knee; and then slowly, exerting all his waning strength, he managed to raise it to his shoulder.

Crump discarded a few pieces of gold and tried again, but with no better success. He cursed the gold, he cursed "Tarzan," he cursed Minsky; and then he took off some more gold and at last succeeded in lifting the heavy burden to his shoulder. He stood there, panting and trembling beneath the hot African sun, the sweat streaming down his forehead into his eyes, into his mouth. He wiped it away and cursed some more.

Minsky started up the trail out of the mine. Every few steps he had to stop and rest. About half way up he fell. He lay where he had fallen, gasping for breath.

Crump was approaching him, cursing and sputtering. "Get out of my way!" he said.

"You aint got here yet," said Minsky, "and I'll lay you a couple of thousand pounds that you don't get here with that load." The words were scarcely out of his mouth when Crump stumbled and fell. He lay there cursing horribly and almost foaming at the mouth.

"You better throw out a couple of race horses and two or three girls," suggested Minsky. "You aint strong enough to carry a racing stable and a whole harem all at the same time."

"If I ever catch up with you, I'm gonna kill you," said Crump.

"Oh, shut up!" said Minsky. "If you'd thought of it, you could have carried your knighthood in that big yap of yours."

Slowly Minsky got to one knee and tried to raise the sack again to get it to his shoulder. It was very heavy, and he knew that even if he succeeded in getting it to his shoulder he could not climb to the top of the excavation with it. Presently he thought of another plan. Still sitting down, he edged up the trail about a foot and then, very laboriously, dragged the coat full of gold after him inch by inch; thus he hitched toward the top, and Crump, seeing that he was succeeding, followed his example.

It took them a long time, and when their great burdens finally lay at the top of the excavation they sprawled beside them to rest.

"I wonder how much we got?" said Crump.

"Maybe a million pounds," said Minsky.

"Maybe two million," suggested Crump.

TWENTY-SEVEN . . Rateng the Hunter

How MANY OF US, farm or city-bound to a hum-drum existence, have longed for adventure, have dreamed of a life close to Nature far from the noise and confusion and problems of civilization, and thrilled to imaginary encounters with wild beasts and savage men whom, by our superior cunning and prowess, we have invariably overcome. Before the radio, or comfortable in a big chair with a good book, we have lived dangerously, albeit vicariously.

Perhaps, after all, this is the best, and it is certainly the safest way to adventure, as Sandra Pickerall doubtless would have assured you as she wandered, lost and hopeless, in the hills of Alemtejo, for it was the longing for adventure which had brought her to Africa with her father. Now, as she searched for a trail from the tableland, she would have given all of the considerable inheritance that would some day have been hers, could she have been safe in Scotland once more.

Rateng, a Galla warrior from the village of Ali the Sultan, was hunting, so far without much success, in fact without any success. It seemed to Rateng that all the game had left the country. He had long ago become disheartened and had turned his steps back toward his village.

Many thoughts passed through the mind of Rateng the hunter as he made his silent way homeward. He wondered what the Alemtejos would do with Ali the Sultan now that they had captured him. Doubtless they would kill him, and then Ali's oldest son would become sultan. Ali was bad enough, thought Rateng, but his son was much worse. Rateng did not like him for many reasons, but the principal one was that he had taken to wife the girl Rateng had desired; then, too, he was haughty and arrogant and a hard taskmaster. When he became sultan he would be a tyrant.

Rateng had been among those who had captured the god and goddess of the Alemtejos in the woods behind the castle;

and he had been with the detachment which escorted them to
the village of Ali the Sultan. Of these things, he thought, too.
He wondered what had become of the white god and goddess,
whom he knew had escaped when the buffaloes and the great
apes and the Alemtejos had attacked the village.

He let his mind dwell upon the white goddess. She had been
very beautiful in her golden dress and breastplates and with
the crown of gold upon her head. If the Alemtejos had not
attacked, she would have been Ali's wife by this time. Rateng
sighed. How nice it must be to be a sultan and have as many
wives as one wished, even including a white goddess; but then
he was not a sultan and he would never have a white wife.
He would be lucky if he had more than one native one.

Though these and many other thoughts ran through the
mind of Rateng the hunter, they did not dim his alertness.
His ears and his eyes were keenly sentient constantly, and
so it was that he heard something approaching from the direction in which he was going.

Rateng grasped his spear more firmly and found concealment behind a low bush. Crouching there he waited, watching,
listening.

Whatever was coming came slowly. Perhaps it was game.
Rateng laid his spear on the ground and fitted an arrow to his
bow, and a moment later there walked into view the white
goddess of whom he had been dreaming.

Rateng caught his breath. What a vision of loveliness she
seemed to him. He noticed how weak she appeared, how faltering her steps; but there was no compassion in the heart of
the Galla. He saw only a woman, and thought only of himself.

As she neared him, he rose up from behind the bush and
confronted her.

Sandra stopped, aghast, and shrank back; and then, motivated solely by terror and without reasoning the futility of her
act, she turned and ran.

Weakened by hunger and exhaustion she took only a few
steps before Rateng overtook her and seized her roughly by
an arm. He whirled her about and held her, looking into
her face.

Rateng's countenance was savage, even by the standards of
savagery. The girl closed her eyes to shut out that cruel,
bestial face.

Rateng had captured the goddess, and he considered the
matter from all angles. The windfall might prove a blessing

or it might prove the reverse. Everything depended upon what advantage he took of his good fortune.

If he took her back to the village, he would not be able to keep her for himself. The sultan's son would take her away from him; and he would get nothing for his pains. Doubtless the Alemtejos would pay a reward for her, if they could get her back in no other way; but if he were to take her to Alemtejo, he was quite sure that his only reward would be slavery for life, unless they chose to sacrifice him to their heathenish god or throw him to the lion devils which they kept at the foot of the great cliff.

There was an alternative, however, a very pleasant-appearing alternative. He knew a place farther back in the hills where there were good water and pleasant fruits, and a snug cave beneath an overhanging rock. There, for a few days, he could make believe that he was a sultan; and when he was ready to go back to the village he could cut the girl's throat and leave her there; and nobody would be any the wiser. This was what Rateng decided to do.

"Are you alone?" he asked in Galla.

"I do not understand," she replied in faltering Swahili.

He repeated the question in that language.

Sandra thought quickly. "I am not alone," she said. "My friends are right behind me. They will be here soon."

Rateng did not believe her, for his keen ears gave him no warning of others nearby; but it was as well to be on the safe side. He had no wish to be robbed of his prize.

"Come," he said, and dragged her off toward the higher hills.

"What do you want of me?" she asked. "What are you going to do with me?"

"You should know," he said. "You are a woman."

"I am not a mortal woman. I am a goddess." She grasped at a straw.

Rateng laughed at her. "There is no God but Allah."

"If you harm me, you will die," she threatened.

"You are an infidel," said Rateng; "and for every infidel I kill, I shall have greater honor in heaven."

"You are going to kill me?" she asked.

"Later," said Rateng.

Until now, Sandra Pickerall thought the worst had befallen her. She had not conceived that there could be anything more. She tried to conjure some plan of escape. If she had her normal strength and vitality she believed she could have outdistanced him in flight; but in her weakened condition, even the thought of it was futile. Self-destruction seemed her only hope; but how was she to destroy herself without the means of destruction? She had no weapon—nothing. Suddenly her eyes fixed themselves upon the quiver of arrows hanging behind the man's naked shoulder. There lay the means, but how was she to take advantage of it?

Rateng grasped her right wrist firmly in his left hand as he dragged her along. She could not reach behind him with her left hand to filch an arrow from the quiver.

Finally, she evolved a plan. She hoped the native would be stupid enough to be taken in. "You do not have to drag me along," she said. "You are hurting my wrist. I will come along with you, for I am too weak to run away."

Rateng grunted and relinquished his hold upon her. "You would not get far," he said; "and if you tried it, I would beat you."

They walked on in silence. Little by little, inch by inch, the girl dropped back until her shoulder was behind the shoulder of the man; then she reached up and took hold of an arrow. She had to be very careful not to warn him by shaking the quiver unnecessarily.

Gently, gradually, she succeeded in withdrawing the arrow from the quiver. Now she held it firmly in her right hand. To thrust the point into her heart would require but an instant of supreme courage. In that instant there raced through her mind a thousand memories of her past life. She thought of her father. He would never know. Doubtless he had long since given her up for dead. No man in all the world, except this native savage, would know of her end or where her bones lay bleaching in the African sun after the hyenas and the jackals and the vultures had torn the flesh away. But she would have to drop farther back before she could accomplish her design, and that might arouse the suspicions of her captor. However, there was no other way. She must take the chance.

She dropped back a little farther. She saw the muscles of the man's shoulder rolling beneath his skin to the swinging of his arm—his left arm. That glossy back, those rolling muscles, fascinated her. Her eyes gleamed at a sudden inspiration. Her mouth went dry at the horror of the thought that filled her mind, but she did not hesitate. She drew back the hand that held the arrow and then, with all her strength, she plunged the missile deep into the body of Rateng the hunter.

With a scream of pain and rage, the savage turned upon her, his face contorted in a horrible grimace of hate and agony. With a wolfish snarl, he leaped upon her, his hands encircling her throat. She stumbled backward and fell, and the man, still clutching her throat, fell upon her.

TWENTY-EIGHT . . Reunited

THE MAN WHO THOUGHT he was Tarzan hunted for food. His heart was heavy with sadness for he believed that the girl he loved was dead. Dutton was dead, too. He had liked Dutton, even though he had been jealous of him. He felt very much alone, for he did not consider Crump and Minsky as companions. He thought of them only with contempt, as he recalled them cursing and quarrelling over their gold. What a contemptible creature man could be, he thought.

He tried to plan, but now there seemed nothing to plan for. He and Sandra and Dutton had been going to escape together. They would have known where to go. He did not. This was the only world he knew. There seemed nothing now for him but to return to Alemtejo. He did not know that Osorio da Serra had seized the kingship from da Gama; and even had he, it would have made no difference, for he knew his hold upon the common people who believed him to be God. In Alemtejo there would be a certain amount of peace and security, with many comforts and good food; but he knew there never could be peace of mind for him, for within him was a restlessness and a questioning that he could not understand. There was always within him the urge to search for something, without knowing what it was for which he searched. It was maddening, this constant groping for this unknowable, unattainable thing.

Of a sudden his melancholy reverie was interrupted by a hoarse and horrible scream. It was the scream of a human being in mortal agony. The man who thought he was Tarzan, motivated by the high humanitarian ideals which he attributed to the ape-man, sprang forward in the direction of the sound, jumping to the conclusion that a human being was being attacked by a wild beast, his heavy Galla spear ready in his hand.

He had covered little more than a hundred yards before

he came upon a sight that filled him with apprehension. He saw the body of Sandra Pickerall lying motionless upon the ground, and, across it, the body of a black Galla warrior from whose back protruded the haft of an arrow. He shot a quick glance in every direction for the enemy that had attacked them, but there was no sign of any enemy; then he ran forward and dragged the body of the Galla from that of the girl. The man was quite dead.

He knelt beside Sandra and raised her in his arms. At first, he detected no sign of life; but as he pressed his ear against her bosom he heard the faint beating of her heart. He chafed her hands and wrists. He held her close to him as though to warm her, oblivious of the fact that the sun was beating down fiercely upon them.

Presently the girl opened her eyes, and they went wide as she looked up into his face. "God!" she said weakly; then she closed her eyes and shuddered and snuggled closer to him. "So this is death!" It was just a breath, almost inaudible, but he caught the words.

"It is not death," he said. "It means life now."

"But you are dead," she said. "I saw the apes kill you, and if we are together again, it must be because I am dead also."

He pressed her closer. "No, my darling," he said, "neither one of us is dead." It was the first time he had ever voiced an expression of endearment to her, but she did not take offense. Instead, she raised her arms and put them about his neck and strained still closer to him.

For a long minute, neither one of them spoke. There was no need of speech. There was perfect understanding without it.

It was the man who broke the silence. "What happened?" he asked. "Who killed him?"

The girl shuddered; then she told him.

"How brave!" he said.

"It was desperation. I was so terribly afraid."

"He must have died almost instantly," said the man.

"Yes. He had his fingers at my throat, but he died before he could close them. The arrow must have pierced his heart." Again she shuddered. "I have killed a man."

"You have killed a beast who would otherwise have killed you. Now we must think about ourselves and try to find a way out of this country."

"Where is Pelham?" she asked. "Did the apes kill him?"

He nodded. "I am afraid so. We found no trace of him. We thought they had killed both him and you. How did you escape?"

She told him briefly of the horrible ordeal she had been through since he had last seen her. "And now," she said, "I suppose we are the only ones left."

"No; Crump and Minsky are still alive. I just left them at the Galla gold mine, loading themselves up with gold they will be unable to carry. I came away to hunt. None of us has eaten much lately, and they are weak from hunger and exhaustion."

"You will have to hunt until you kill something then," she said, "and take it back to them."

"No," he said emphatically. "They are not worth saving, though if I were alone I should have found food for them; but I'll never expose you to those two. They are the worst blackguards I have ever seen."

"You will leave them to die?" she asked.

"They have their gold," he said. "That is what they wished more than anything else in the world. They should die happy."

"What are we to do?" she asked.

"We could go back to Alemtejo and be God and Goddess again," he said, "or I can take you down over the cliff and try to return you to your father."

"Oh, I don't know," she said. "I want so to live, now that there is so much to live for."

"We shall live," he said, "and we shall be happy. I know it."

"Well what must we do?" she asked. "You decide, and I'll do anything you say."

"We'll tackle the cliff," he said.

With the man at her side, Sandra seemed to have acquired new strength. Much of her fatigue and exhaustion dropped from her, and she walked along at his side as they started down out of the hills toward the plain across which lay Alemtejo and the mighty barrier cliff.

Later in the afternoon he brought down a small buck with a lucky shot.

The animal had been drinking at a tiny stream, so now they had both food and water; and after a short search, the man found a little glade hidden away in a ravine where they might camp in comparative safety.

"We'll stay here," he said, "until you have regained your strength. You couldn't travel far in the condition you're in now. We've water and meat, and there's edible fruit on some of those trees."

He busied himself butchering the buck; and when that was done, he gathered firewood, and after many futile attempts finally succeeded in coaxing a blaze by the primitive method of twirling a pointed stick in a tinder-filled hole in another piece of wood. As the first thin wisp of smoke arose, the girl clapped her hands.

"Marvelous!" she exclaimed. "I thought you'd never be able to do it; and as hungry as I am, I don't believe I could have eaten raw meat."

He grilled some of the meat on sharpened sticks. It was partly raw and partly charred; but when it was cool enough to eat without burning them, they ate it ravenously; and when they had eaten they went to the stream and, lying on their bellies, drank as the beasts drink.

The girl rolled over on her back in the deep grass, cupping her hands beneath her head. "I never expected to feel so happy and contented and safe again," she said. "It's perfect here."

"It would be perfect for me anywhere with you," he replied.

"Maybe that's what makes it perfect for both of us," she said, "just being together; and to think that just a little while ago, I feared and hated you."

He nodded. "You had reason," he said.

"And that even now I don't know your name, nor who you are, nor where you come from."

"You know as much as I do," he said.

"Do you suppose some day we'll know?" she asked.

He shrugged. "What difference does it make? We know we love each other. Is not that enough?"

The sun set; and, in the distance, a lion roared.

TWENTY-NINE . . Gold and Death

CRUMP AND MINSKY LAY where they had fallen at the edge of the workings, too weak and exhausted to rise. Each clutched his bundle of gold, as though fearful someone might try to steal it from him. For some time they lay gasping beneath the pitiless sun; then Minsky raised himself on one elbow and looked around. He saw a tree nearby that cast a little shade, and laboriously he dragged himself and his horde of golden wealth toward it.

"What you doin'?" demanded Crump.

"Huntin' shade," replied Minsky. "I can't lie out in that sun no longer."

Crump raised himself and hitched along in the direction of the tree, dragging his load with him; and at last they were both in the shade.

"If we rest a few minutes," said Crump, "we ought to be able to get goin'."

"I aint goin' no place 'til that guy comes back with food," said Minsky. "If we get a little grub under our belts, it'll put some pep in us."

The afternoon wore on. The two men were suffering from thirst; but now they were afraid to leave for fear the hunter would return with food and they would miss him.

Night fell. "What do you suppose has become of that damned ape-man?" asked Crump. "He oughta been back a long while ago."

"Maybe he aint comin' back," said Minsky.

"Why shouldn't he?" demanded Crump.

"Why should he?" asked Minsky. "We don't mean nothing to him. What can we do for him? And he aint got no reason to be in love with us."

"If I ever lay my hands on him, I'll kill him," said Crump.

"Oh, nuts!" growled Minsky. "You're always gonna kill

139

somebody. You won't never kill anybody now, 'cause you aint got no gun to shoot 'em in the back with."

Crump mumbled beneath his breath; and for a long time there was silence, which was broken finally by Minsky's stertorous breathing. He slept.

Crump half raised himself on an elbow and looked in the direction of his companion. He cursed himself because he was not strong enough to carry both loads of gold, for he was thinking how easy it would be to kill Minsky while he slept; but what was the use? He couldn't even carry his own load. Maybe later, when they had had food and water and regained strength, he would have another opportunity.

"Two million pounds," he murmured before he fell into the sleep of exhaustion.

When morning came, the two men felt somewhat refreshed and much stronger than they had the afternoon before. They had given up any hope that the hunter would return, and Crump wasted a great deal of breath cursing him.

Minsky said nothing. He was the more intelligent of the two, and by far the more dangerous. Someday he would meet the ape-man, he thought, some day when Minsky carried his favorite weapon, the trigger of which he could almost feel beneath his finger.

Presently he cast these thoughts from his mind, and spoke. "We better be movin'," he said. "We gotta find water. We can get along for awhile without food, but we gotta have water."

The two men rose and laboriously raised their packs to their shoulders; and then, Minsky in the lead, they staggered back down the trail that led away from the Galla mine.

At first, in the cool of the morning, they got along fairly well, though they often staggered and sometimes almost fell; but when the sun rose higher and beat down upon them, they suffered the agonies of thirst; yet they kept doggedly on.

"There's gotta be water! There's gotta be water!" mumbled Crump, and he kept on repeating it over and over again.

"Shut up!" growled Minsky.

"There's gotta be water! There's gotta be water!" croaked Crump.

The interminable day dragged slowly on to the tempo of their shuffling, heavy feet; and there was no water. A gloating Nemesis, the implacable sun burned through their helmets, through their skulls, through their brains, conjuring weird visions and hallucinations. Repeatedly, Crump tried to swallow, but there was no saliva in his mouth, and the muscles of his throat refused to respond to his will. They no longer perspired. They were dried-out husks, animated only by a desire to live and by greed. It was difficult to say which of these two motivating forces was the stronger, which they would fight for longer—their gold or their lives.

Through cracked and swollen lips, Crump babbled of his past life, of his "old woman," of food and of drink, of the men he had killed, and the girls he had had. Presently he commenced to laugh, a dry, cackling laugh.

Minsky looked at him. "Shut up!" he snarled. "You're goin' nuts."

"Sir Thomas Crump," mumbled Crump. "That's what I am—Sir Thomas Crump; and you're my man. Hi, Minsky, fetch me monocle and me slippers. I'm going to call on the king, and have steak-and-kidney pie and four gallons of water—water—water!"

"Plumb daffy," muttered Minsky.

For a time they plodded on in silence, always straining their eyes ahead for some sign of water. Minsky felt his mind wandering. At various times he saw streams, and pools, and once a lake where boats sailed; but he knew they were hallucinations, and each time with an effort of will he snapped back to normal.

They were weakening rapidly. Every few minutes they were forced to stop and rest; but they did not dare lay down their burdens, for they knew they would not have the strength to raise them again. They just stood for a minute or two, swaying and panting, and then once more took up the agonizing struggle.

Minsky, the stronger and more determined, was some hundred feet ahead of Crump when he stumbled against a rock, hidden in the grass, and fell. He did not try to rise immediately, for, being down, he decided to lie there for a few minutes and rest.

Crump staggered forward a few steps toward Minsky. "Don't drink it all," he cried. "Leave some for me, you swine!" He thought Minsky, lying on his stomach with his face against the ground, had found water. He had to stop and rest again. Each time he planted a foot, he could scarcely raise it from the ground without falling. He weaved from side to side, and forward and back, trying to maintain his balance; then he lurched forward a few more steps. At last he reached Minsky, and, dropping to his knees, fell forward on his face searching for the water. He began to curse horribly, applying every opprobrious epithet to Minsky to which he could lay his tongue. "You drunk it all up," he croaked. "You drunk it all up. You didn't leave me a drop."

"There wasn't no water," said Minsky. "I just fell down. I stubbed my toe. I'm gonna lie here and rest a few minutes."

Crump made no reply; but presently he commenced to sob. "I thought there was water," he blubbered.

For half an hour they lay where they had fallen, the sun taking its toll of what little strength remained to them; then Minsky started to rise. "We'd better be movin'," he said. "I think I've been hearin' somethin'."

"What?" asked Crump.

"Water," said Minsky. "I can hear it runnin'. It's in the bottom of this here ravine right in front of us."

Crump listened intently. "Yes," he said, "I hear it, too. We couldn't both be wrong"; nor were they, for just a few yards ahead of them, at the bottom of a shallow ravine, a little stream ran down toward the plain, splashing over the rocks and gravel of its bed.

Minsky started to rise. "We can leave the gold here," he said, "and come back for it." Laboriously he sought to raise his body from the ground, but his arms gave beneath him and he sank back upon his face; then Crump tried to rise. He got to his knees, but he could get no farther. "Get up, my man," he said to Minsky, "and fetch me water."

"Go to hell," said Minsky. "Get up yourself"; but, nevertheless, he tried again to rise, and again he sank back, defeated.

Crump struck him. "Get up, you fool," he cried, "and get water, or we'll both die."

Again Minsky made the effort. Crump tried to help him, pulling on the back of his shirt; and at last Minsky came to his knees. He tried to get one of his feet beneath him; but the effort caused him to lose his balance, and he fell over upon his side.

"Get up! Get up, you swine!" shrieked Crump.

"I can't," said Minsky.

"Yes, you can." Crump's voice was a rasping scream. "Yes, you can. You're just lyin' there waitin' for me to die, so you can get my gold; but I'll show you, I'll show you, you'll never have it." He turned and rummaged in his coat until he had located a large piece of virgin gold. He leaned over Minsky, the great shining lump of metal in his hand.

Minsky lay upon his side as he had fallen. "You won't never get mine," said Crump; "but I'll get yours." He raised the lump of gold and brought it down heavily upon Minsky's temple. The man quivered convulsively and lay still.

"That'll learn you," growled Crump, and struck again; then, in a sudden frenzy of maniacal fury, he crashed the metal again and again upon the other's skull, reducing it to a bloody pulp of bone and brain.

He sat back on his haunches and surveyed his handiwork. He commenced to laugh. "I told you I'd kill you," he said. "The next time I tell you, you'll believe me." He had gone completely mad.

"Now I'll have it all, yours and mine."

Somehow he got to his knees and, seizing Minsky's horde of gold, he tried to raise it to his shoulder, but he could not even lift it from the ground. Again and again he tried, but each time he was weaker, and at last he turned and threw himself upon his own gold. Clutching at it with greedy fingers, he commenced to sob.

In the ravine, the little stream, cold and clear, shimmered and played in the sunlight.

THIRTY . . Our First Home

TARZAN HAD BEEN IN NO HURRY to find the easier trail that led down from the plateau of Alemtejo. There was another matter of greater importance, the finding of the man who had stolen his name and brought it into disrepute; also, there was the matter of food. Observation had assured him that there was little or no game to be found in the foothills or on the plain; and so he had determined to go farther back into the hills, for he and Chilton must eat.

More than anything else, Chilton was interested in getting out of the country; but he soon discovered that he had no voice in the matter, unless he chose to go alone. It was Tarzan who made all the decisions; and whatever he did, he did without haste. Chilton thought he was lazy, but Chilton had never seen him act in an emergency.

In many ways, he reminded Chilton of a wild beast, particularly of a lion. Lions move slowly with a certain lazy majesty. They are unconscious of the passage of time; but Chilton knew that when a lion was aroused, he was a very different creature, and he wondered if the analogue would hold good if Tarzan were aroused.

The hunting carried them some distance back into the hills, but it proved successful, and they had flesh to eat along with the fruits and vegetables which Tarzan gathered.

The ape-man had divided his kill, giving half of it to Chilton and the latter was more than a little horrified when he saw his companion carry his share off to a little distance, and, squatting upon his haunches, tear the raw meat with his teeth like a wild beast; but he was still more horrified when he heard the low growls rumbling from the ape-man's chest, the while he fed.

Chilton eyed the great hunk of raw meat in his own hands. Finally he ventured a remark. "I say, you know, I don't think I can stomach this raw."

"Cook it," said Tarzan

"But we have no matches," demurred Chilton.

"Gather some wood," directed the ape-man. "I'll make fire for you."

The next day they wandered about, quite aimlessly, Chilton thought; but it was not aimless wandering insofar as Tarzan was concerned. Whenever he went into a new country he studied it, for he might have to return. He noted every landmark and he never forgot one. He discovered where the water lay and which way the wind blew, and the nature of the game and where it might be found. Tarzan might seem lazy and indifferent to Chilton, but that was because the man was not familiar with the ways of Tarzan or other wild beasts.

They were working down through the foothills toward the plain, when Tarzan suddenly stopped, instantly alert.

Chilton stopped, too, and looked around. "Do you see something?" he asked.

"There is a white man over there," said Tarzan, "and he is dead."

"I don't see anything." said Chilton.

"Neither do I," said Tarzan, as he started off in the direction he had indicated.

Chilton was puzzled. It meant nothing to him that a gentle breeze was blowing directly into his face. He wondered if his companion were not a little balmy, and he would like to have wagered a few pounds that there was no dead man there. If it were Rand, now, he could get a bet. Rand was always keen to bet on anything.

Presently they topped a little rise, and below them, near the edge of the ravine, they saw the bodies of two men. Chilton's eyes went wide. "I say," he said, "how did you know?"

"By training that is not included in the curriculum of either Oxford or Cambridge," replied the ape-man, with a faint smile.

"Wherever you learned it, it's most extraordinary," said Chilton.

They stopped beside the two men, and Tarzan stood looking down upon them. "Both dead," he said. "They died of thirst and exhaustion." He stooped and examined their packs.

"Gold!" exclaimed Chilton. "My word, what a lot of it; and look at the size of those nuggets. They're not nuggets, they're chunks, chunks, of pure gold."

"The price of two worthless lives," said the ape-man; "but quite typical of civilized man that they should have died within a few yards of water rather than abandon their gold."

"They would have been better off in Alemtejo," said Chilton.

"It is better that two such scoundrels are dead," replied Tarzan.

"You knew them before?" asked Chilton.

"I knew them. This one tried to kill me." He touched Crump's body with his foot.

Chilton stopped and hefted the two bundles of gold. "Quite a neat little fortune, what?" he said.

Tarzan shrugged. "Would you like to carry it out with you?" he asked.

"And end up like this?" Chilton pointed to the two men. "Thanks; but I have all I need, if I can ever get out to it."

"Then let's be going," said the ape-man.

* * *

The sun shining on her face half awakened Sandra, but she did not open her eyes. She had been dreaming of home, and she thought she was in her bed in her father's house. Presently it occurred to her that her bed was very hard, and she opened her eyes to look up into a blue sky. She was still not fully awake as she looked to her left and saw hills, and trees, and a little stream. For a moment she thought she was dreaming; and then she turned her head in the other direction and saw a sleeping man lying a short distance away; then she remembered, and momentarily her heart sank. It was as though she had suddenly been snatched away from home into a strange world, a savage, dangerous world; but as her eyes lingered upon the man, she became content; and she thought, better here with him than anywhere else in the world without him.

She rose silently and went to the little brook and drank; then she washed her hands and face in the clear, cold water. She recalled she had heard a lion roar the night before and that she had been afraid; but she had been so exhausted she had fallen asleep in the face of the menace the roar had connoted.

She would have been surprised and terrified, too, now, could she have known that the lion had come to the opposite side of the brook during the night and stood there looking at them as they lay in the moonlight. He had stood there a long time watching them; and then he had turned and moved majestically away, for the scent of a white was unfamiliar to his nostrils, and wild beasts are wary of things with which they are not familiar; then, too, he had not been ravenously hungry.

When she turned around again, the man was sitting up looking at her; and they exchanged good mornings.

"You slept well?" he asked.

"Yes; and I am so very much rested."

"That is good, but we'll stay here today and give you a chance to recuperate your strength."

She looked around. "It's heavenly here," she said. "I almost wish we could stay forever. It is the first time in weeks that I have felt secure and have been happy."

They spent the day resting and talking, they had so much to talk about. She told him of her home, of the mother she had lost when she was a little girl, and of the father whose pal she had been ever since.

He could go back only two years to the day he had found himself in the castle of Alemtejo; beyond that, he knew nothing. Of the future, there was little to say other than to compare hopes.

"One of the first things we'll do," she told him, "is to find out who you are. I know one thing about you for sure, and of another I am almost equally certain."

"What, for instance?" he asked.

"Well, I know you are a gentleman."

"Do gentlemen steal girls and carry them off into captivity?" he asked.

"That was not you, not the real you," she defended him.

"I hope not," he said. "Now, what was the other thing you think you know about me?"

"I am certain that you are an American. I have known many of them from all parts of America; and you have a soft drawl that is typical of people who live in the Southern states."

He shook his head. "I have given up trying to remember. Sometimes I thought I should go crazy trying to force myself to recall something of my past life. Maybe, if I do recall it, I shall wish I hadn't. Suppose that I were a criminal, a fugitive from justice? For all you know, I may be a murderer or thief, or for all I know either."

"It will make no difference to me," she said.

He took her in his arms and kissed her.

"I shall hate to leave this spot," she said; "but always I shall carry the picture of it in my mind."

"And I, too," he replied. "Our first home! but tomorrow we must leave it and go down out of the hills."

THIRTY-ONE . . "I Am Going to Kill You"

THE NEXT MORNING WHEN Chilton awoke, he found himself alone. He looked around but found no sign of his erstwhile companion. "I wonder if the blighter has deserted me," he soliloquized. "He didn't seem that sort; but then there's never any telling. These wild men are all a bit balmy, I'm told. Anyway, why shouldn't he go on his own? I'm not much use to him. He has to feed me and find water for me; and I rather imagine he'd have to protect me, if we got in trouble. Of course, I might find the trail out for him; but after being with him as long as I have, I rather imagine he can find it himself if he wants to. There doesn't seem to be anything about this blooming country that chap doesn't know."

He looked around again rather anxiously. "I say, Tarzan, or whatever your name is where the devil are you?" he shouted. "It's going to be beastly embarrassing to be left here alone," he thought.

Presently he heard a noise behind him, and turning suddenly he recognized the ape-man who was carrying a young wild pig and some fruit. Chilton breathed a sigh of relief, but he said nothing to Tarzan of his fears.

"You had good luck," said Chilton, nodding toward the pig.

"I had better luck than this, I think," said Tarzan. "I got to thinking last night about those two men we found yesterday, and it occurred to me that possibly they might prove a clue to the whereabouts of the man I am looking for; so I went back there to backtrack their trail."

"You don't mean to say you've been way back there this morning?" demanded Chilton.

"I've been considerably farther; but I left here a couple of hours before dawn. It was light shortly after I reached them, and I followed their trail back until I found the trail of a white man leading off toward the west. He was barefooted, the man who made the trail. There are very few white men in this part of the country and none, I think, other than myself and this impostor, who goes without boots. The trail was a couple of days old, but it is all I need. Now I know I shall soon find him and kill him. As soon as we have eaten, we'll go back and pick up that trail."

"You don't really have to kill him, do you?" demanded Chilton. "That seems beastly cold-blooded."

"Why shouldn't I kill him?" asked Tarzan.

"Perhaps he had a good reason. Perhaps he can explain."

"How can he explain stealing my name and the women and children of my friends?" demanded the ape-man. "If I find him, he'll have to talk very fast. He'll have to say all he is ever going to say in the time it will take my arrow to reach him from the moment I lay my eyes upon him."

"Oh, after all, my dear fellow, you can't do that, you know. It isn't done. It isn't human. Civilized men don't do things like that."

"You are not talking to a civilized man," replied Tarzan.

"Yes," said Chilton, "I was afraid of that."

Hyenas were tearing at the bodies of Crump and Minsky when the two men reached them. The sight shocked and sickened Chilton; but Tarzan of the Apes strode by with scarcely a glance.

Presently they came to the spoor Tarzan was to follow, and turned to the left. Chilton saw no evidence that anyone had ever passed that way before; but Tarzan followed the spoor at a long, swinging stride, never losing it.

They had continued for almost an hour when Tarzan suddenly stopped, and Chilton could see that he was listening intently. "Someone is coming," he said presently. "I'll go ahead. You can follow on, slowly." Then he was off with a swinging trot that covered the ground rapidly.

"Most amazing person," sighed Chilton. "Can't see anyone, can't hear anyone. How in the devil does he know there is anyone? But at that I'll bet he's right. Most extraordinary, though, most extraordinary."

Tarzan moved rapidly and silently toward the sound he had heard. At first it had been but a faint suggestion of a sound which overrode the rustling of the leaves and the humming of insects. It came to Tarzan's ears, though, as the sound of human voices. It puzzled him, however, because the spoor he was following was the spoor of a single person; and, as yet, he was too far away to in any way identify the voices, which might have been those of black men or of white. All that he was positive of was that they were voices.

Sandra and the man who thought he was Tarzan walked hand-in-hand down toward the floor of the vallley. They were happy. It seemed to Sandra that such happiness never could be blasted. She was ebullient with optimism and hope. Perhaps it was the natural reaction after so many weeks of homelessness, or perhaps she chose to ignore the possibilities of the future. It was enough that she was with the man she loved. It was well she could not know that coming silently through the jungle was a man endowed with all the savageness of a wild beast, coming nearer and nearer with murder in his heart, to kill this man.

And then, of a sudden, he stood before them. "Tarzan!" she exclaimed. "Oh, Tarzan, I thought you were dead."

The ape-man made no reply. His cold grey eyes were fixed upon the man who said he was Tarzan. He had never seen him before; but he did not need to ask if he were the man he sought. His garb told him that, as well as the fact he was with the girl he had stolen.

Tarzan came quite close and stopped. He tossed his weapons to the ground. "Throw down your bow and your spear," he said.

The other looked puzzled. "Why?" he asked.

"Because I am going to kill you; but I will give you your chance."

The other threw down his weapons. "I don't know why you want to kill me," he said; "but you are at liberty to try." He showed no fear.

"I am going to kill you because you stole my name, and stole the women and children of my friends. You either killed them or carried them into slavery. My friends think it was I; and they have turned against me. Now I kill!"

Suddenly Sandra stepped between the two men, facing Tarzan. "You must listen to me," she said. "You must not kill this man."

Tarzan looked at her in surprise. "Why not?" he demanded. "Besides what he did to me, he stole you and took you into captivity. For that alone, he should be killed."

"You don't understand," said Sandra. "Please listen. This man is not a bad man. Something has happened to him. He has lost his memory. He does not know who he is; but I have convinced him that he is not Tarzan. He was forced to do the things he did by Cristoforo da Gama, King of Alemtejo. You must believe me. This man is a gentleman and a good man."

"Is that all?" demanded Tarzan.

"No," said the girl.

"What else, then?"

"I love him."

Tarzan turned to the man. "What have you to say?" he demanded.

"Miss Pickerall speaks the truth. I do not know who I am. Until she told me differently, I really thought I was Tarzan of the Apes. I did not know that the things I did were wrong. Now, I am trying to make amends. I am trying to take Miss Pickerall back to her father. I cannot bring back to life those whose death I caused, nor can I free those whom I took into slavery. I wish that I could."

Tarzan had been watching the man intently and now he stood in silence for a moment regarding him; then he stooped and picked up his weapons. He was an excellent judge of character and he believed the man.

"Very well," he said. "I will help you to take Miss Pickerall back to her father. He will decide what is to be done to you."

The other inclined his head. "That is satisfactory to me," he said. "All I care about is getting her back safely."

"Now I know we are going to be all right," said Sandra to the ape-man, "now that you are with us."

"Where are the rest of your party?" asked Tarzan.

"Pelham Dutton was killed by great apes a couple of days ago," replied the girl. "The others I have not seen for a long time."

"Crump and Minsky are dead," said Tarzan. "I found their bodies yesterday. They died of thirst and exhaustion."

"We are the only ones left," said the man who had called himself Tarzan.

"Look!" exclaimed Sandra, pointing. "Someone is coming. Who is that?"

THIRTY-TWO . . Rand

FRANCIS BOLTON-CHILTON plodded along in the direction Tarzan had taken, but none too sure that it was the right direction. He had no wood-craft. Tarzan's spoor would have been plain to Tarzan and to any other denizen of the jungle. There were no trails here. It was an open wood with practically no underbrush.

"How does the bally wildman expect me to follow him?" muttered Chilton. "He just says, 'Follow me,' and ups and disappears. Most extraordinary fellow I ever saw, but a good sort even if he is a little balmy, running around in a bloomin' G-string, eating his meat raw, and growling like a lion in a zoo while he eats it. Sometimes he gives me the creeps; but, by gad, he inspires confidence. Somehow I feel safe when he's around, even though I never know what minute he may jump on me and bite a steak out of me. Most absurd, what?"

By accident, he stumbled upon the two men and the girl. "My word," he exclaimed, "two of them!" as he saw another man garbed exactly as Tarzan was.

When Sandra exclaimed and pointed, Tarzan turned and saw Bolton-Chilton approaching. "My friend," he said simply.

When Bolton-Chilton came closer and got a better look at the man who had called himself Tarzan, he hurried toward him with extended hand. "My word! Rand!" he exclaimed. "This is wonderful, old fellow. I thought you dead for the last two years."

The man he had called Rand knitted his brows in puzzlement and shook his head. "You must be mistaken," he said. "I never saw you before."

Chilton dropped his hand to his side. "What!" he exclaimed. "You mean to say that you don't remember me? I'm Francis—Francis Bolton-Chilton."

The other shook his head. "I never heard the name before," he said.

Sandra turned to Bolton-Chilton. "Do you know him?" she asked eagerly.

"Of course I know him," said Chilton. "What the devil does he mean by saying he doesn't know me? I can't understand it."

"Something has happened to him," said Sandra. "He recalls nothing except what has happened during the last two years. Tell him who he is."

"He is Colin T. Randolph, Jr., an American from West Virginia."

"There, you see I was right," said Sandra to Rand. "I told you you were an American from the South."

"Where have you been all this time?" demanded Chilton.

"In Alemtejo," replied Rand. "You are sure you know who I am? There can be no mistake?"

"Absolutely none, my boy."

A look of relief came into Rand's eyes. "It is something to know that somebody knows who I am, even if I can't remember," he said. "Maybe it will come back to me some time."

"You know all about him?" asked Sandra.

"Pretty much everything there is to know. We flew together in Spain for a year. Men get pretty close under circumstances like that, you know, and talk a lot about home and their past lives. Say, I even know the names of the servants in his father's home, although I have never been there; and Rand knew as much about me before—before this happened."

"Then you know—" she hesitated. "You'd know if—if—" she stopped short.

"If what?" asked Bolton-Chilton.

"Is he married?" she asked in a very faint voice.

Bolton-Chilton smiled and shook his head. "No, my dear young lady," he said, "not unless he has married within the last two years."

"I just thought he ought to know," said Sandra lamely.

"Yes, it's quite customary for one to know if he's married," agreed Chilton.

Tarzan had been an interested auditor. He was glad that the girl's belief had been substantiated and he was still more glad he had not killed the man; but now that the mystery was on the way to being cleared up, there was a more important thing to consider. He was faced with the responsibility of getting three people out of one hostile country and through another before any of them could be even remotely considered safe, and he wanted to get it over with. "Come," he said, "let's be moving."

"Where to?" asked Rand.

"There is supposed to be an easy trail leading out of this valley. I am looking for it."

"So were we," said Rand.

Tarzan moved at a brisk pace and there was little opportunity for conversation until they made camp that night. It was cool, and they built a fire and gathered around it to roast bits of the meat that Chilton and Tarzan had brought with them from the kill Tarzan had made the previous day.

Sandra had been fairly consumed with curiosity all during the march to hear more about Colin T. Randolph, Jr., from the lips of Bolton-Chilton. So she sat very close to the man who had thought he was Tarzan. "Rand," she said. "You don't know how wonderful it is to have a name for you. Do you know that during all the time I have known you I have never called you anything?"

"Well, you were sure I wasn't Tarzan, and maybe you were equally sure I was not God."

"Quite," she agreed; "but now that I know who you are, I want to know what you are and all about you." She turned to Bolton-Chilton. "Won't you tell me," she asked, "all that you know—how he got here and all of that?"

"Gladly," said the Englishman. "You see, as I told you, Rand and I flew together in Spain. Finally, we got fed up with the slaughter and quit; and Rand stopped in England with me on his way back to America.

"There's one thing you ought to know about Rand. He's an inveterate gambler. I don't mean with cards, or dice, or anything like that. I mean he is always betting on something. He'd bet £20 that one raindrop would reach the bottom of a pane of glass before another raindrop. Before he'd take off for a raid, he'd bet he would return or he'd bet he wouldn't return. You could take your choice. He would bet on anything either way, just so he could get a bet. That's why he's here; that's why I'm here; and evidently that's why you are here."

"And why I'm here," said Tarzan.

"But I can't see what that's got to do with it," said Sandra. "He certainly didn't bet that he would come to Africa and abduct me. He'd never even heard of me."

"I'll try to explain," said Bolton-Chilton; "but I'll have

to go back a little. You see, Rand used to talk a lot about Tarzan of the Apes. It was a regular obsession with him. He said he had read so much about him for years and had admired him so much that he decided to emulate him; so he learned to do as many of the things Tarzan did as he was able. He developed his physique until he was as strong as a young bull and as agile as a cat. He practiced at archery until he was pretty good with a bow and arrow. He told me that he used to win all the tournaments he entered.

"It was his ambition to come to Africa and try living like Tarzan; and I used to kid him a lot about it and tell him he'd starve to death in a week if he were set down in central Africa alone, that is, if some lion didn't get him before he starved; but he'd never admit there was a chance of either one or the other. Of course, it was all kidding, and neither one of us ever thought he would really try it. It helped to pass the time away when we weren't in the air."

Rand was as interested a listener as Sandra or Tarzan, for to him the story was as new. His brows were knit in an effort to recall. Sandra noticed the strained expression in his eyes and placed her hand on his. "Relax," she said. "It will all come back to you some day. Don't try to force it."

"It makes a good story about somebody else," he said with a wry smile; "but if it is I he is talking about, it makes me appear something of a silly ass."

"Not at all," said Chilton. "You were anything but that; and since I have met the real Tarzan, I think you were pretty bright in trying to emulate him,"

"Go on with the story," said Sandra. "How did it all lead up to this?"

"Well, after we got back to England," continued Bolton-Chilton, "we were sitting around my club one day, reading the papers, when Rand ran across a story from South Africa about a native boy who had been captured with a band of baboons. He acted just like them and ran around on all fours most of the time; and he didn't know a word of any language, unless it were baboon talk, if there is such a thing, 'There,' said Rand, showing me the article, 'that proves my point. If that kid could do it, I could do it.'

" 'But he was a native, and he didn't know any other kind of life. If the baboons took him in at all, they would have fed him and protected him. You'd be on your own. No, you never could do it. You wouldn't last a week,' I told him.

" 'A thousand pounds says that I can,' said Rand.

"So I took him up. We argued the thing for an hour, and the bet finally simmered down to this: I was to fly him to Central Africa; and after we had found a place in good game country where we could land, I was to leave him and pick him up in a month. He was to dress as Tarzan dressed and carry only the same weapons that Tarzan carried. Every few days, however, I was to fly over the district where he was; and if he were alive, he'd signal me with smoke from a fire—one smoke column, he was O.K.—two smoke columns, he needed help. If he stuck it out a month, he collected £1000. If he didn't, I collected the same amount.

"We took off in Rand's ship, and everything went lovely at first. As we neared the point where we wanted to commence looking for a landing place, Rand changed into his Tarzan outfit—loin-cloth, knife, rope, bow and arrows, and the rest of it.

"We ran into some pretty rough country with mountains and low clouds. It didn't look so good, for there was no place to land and the clouds seemed to be settling lower; so we decided to get above them. It was awful thick and we were flying blind, with every once in awhile a mountain peak sticking its nose up too close for comfort; then, all of a sudden, our motor quit.

"Rand told me to jump. There wasn't anything else for it. It would have been suicide to try to make a deadstick landing under the circumstances; so I jumped, and that's the last I saw of Rand until today. That was two years ago.

"I came down on an open tableland not far from a native village. I stayed where I was for awhile watching for Rand to come down; but he didn't come; and then I made my way to the village. It was the village of Ali the Sultan; and I have been there ever since, a slave, working part of the time in the most fabulous goldmine I have ever seen or heard of. Well, that's about all there is to my story."

"And what about you, Rand?" asked Sandra. "Does this recall anything to your mind?"

"It only explains how I got to Alemtejo," replied Rand. "They said I came down out of the sky; so I must have bailed out and landed near da Gama's castle; but I don't remember anything about it. I've got to take Bolton-Chilton's word for it; but it is all very puzzling. I don't know the first thing about flying a ship."

Bolton-Chilton shook his head. "Perhaps you don't now," he said; "but you were one of the best pilots I ever saw."

"I wonder what became of the ship?" said Sandra.

"It must have crashed somewhere near Alemtejo," suggested Bolton-Chilton.

"If it had, I should have heard of it," said Rand, "and none of the Alemtejos ever reported anything like that."

"Just another mystery," said Sandra.

THIRTY-THREE . . A Ship

THE FOLLOWING MORNING THEY STARTED down toward the plain in search of the trail to the low country. On the way, they passed the scattered bones of Crump and Minsky now picked almost clean by hyenas, jackals and vultures. They paused a moment to contemplate the two packs of gold which had contributed so greatly to the deaths of these men. Chilton helfted first one hoard and then the other. "Must be between £25,000 and £50,000," he said. "Quite a neat little fortune."

"Well, I guess it'll have to stay here for the Gallas or the Alemtejos," said Rand.

They continued on then, without regret, down toward the plain. They never found the trail that the Gallas and the Alemtejo's knew; and they were miles from it when they came to a long, level shelf several hundred feet below the level of the main plateau. It was a treeless stretch perhaps a mile in length and half that in width, covered deeply with lush grasses. It lay far off the beaten track of either Galla or Alemtejo and had, perhaps, never been trod by the foot of man before.

Tarzan, who was in the lead when they came in sight of it, stopped and pointed. "Look!" he said, "a ship."

The others clustered about him excitedly. "What luck!" exclaimed Sandra. "Perhaps he can take us all out."

"By jove!" exclaimed Bolton-Chilton. "It can't be—it can't be possible; but if that isn't Rand's plane, I'll eat it. I'd know it as far as I could see it."

"It doesn't seem possible," said Sandra, "for that ship certainly never crashed."

"Let's get down there and have a look at it," said Bolton-Chilton. "Be most extraordinary if we could fly it out, wouldn't it?"

"Not much chance of that," said Sandra, "after it has

158

stood out in all sorts of weather for two years. The fabric would be pretty well shot."

"Wouldn't have hurt it a bit," Bolton-Chilton assured her. "It's an all-metal plane."

It took them nearly an hour to clamber down to the shelf and make their way to the ship. "It's Rand's all right," said Bolton-Chilton; "and from here it looks as airworthy as ever. It doesn't look as though even the landing gear were damaged." And when they reached it, they found he was right. The tires were flat, but otherwise it seemed to be in perfect condition.

"Rand must have landed it," said Sandra; "but of course he's forgotten."

"I don't think I landed it," said Rand, "because the Alemtejo all insisted that I came down out of the sky, that is, that I floated down all by myself."

"The ship landed itself," said Bolton-Chilton. "Of course, it's most unusual, but not without precedent. I remember reading of a couple of army fliers bailing out somewhere in California, a number of years ago. Their plane made a perfect landing by itself; and the pilot was court-martialed."

Colin T. Randolph, Jr., walked all around his plane, examining it from every angle, an eager light in his eyes; then he clambered to the wing and entered the cabin, followed by the others. He entered the pilot's compartment and sat down in the pilot's seat. He examined the instrument board, running his hands over it caressingly. He grasped the wheel, gripping it so hard that his knuckles showed white. Suddenly he relaxed and turned toward them, tears in his eyes. "Oh, Sandra! Sandra! It's all right now. I remember everything." She came and stood beside him, but emotion choked whatever words were on her lips.

"I say," said Bolton-Chilton, "isn't this great? It just needed something like this to jar your memory loose, something you had loved a lot in your other life; and you certainly loved this ship."

"I remember now," said Rand slowly. "I stayed with the ship about five minutes after you bailed out; then I jumped. I came down in the ballium of the castle of Alemtejo. I can see it all plainly now—that amazing castle here in the wilderness, and the strange little brown men with golden cuirasses standing gaping up at me. I was swinging badly; and just before I landed, I crashed against the castle wall. It must have been that that knocked me cuckoo."

"Do you suppose she'll fly?" asked Sandra.

"If she won't, we'll make her," said Rand.

While the others pumped up the tires, praying fervently that they would hold, Rand disassembled the carburetor, found the trouble, and corrected it.

There followed inspection and lubrication; and two hours later, they sat tensely in the cabin, each holding his breath, as Rand prepared to start the engine.

Almost instantly they were rewarded with the roar of propeller and exhaust.

"Now if those tires will hold," said Rand. "Perhaps you'd all better get out and let me try it alone."

"No," said Sandra, "not I"; nor would Tarzan nor Bolton-Chilton desert him.

Rand taxied along the shelf and turned back into the wind. "If you want to take that gold out," said Tarzan, "now you have the means. There's a place to land not far from where Crump and Minsky died."

"Not I," said Bolton-Chilton. "I have all I need; so has Rand; and I'm quite sure that the daughter of Timothy Pickerall doesn't need any more; but how about you, Tarzan?"

Tarzan smiled. "What would I do with gold?" he asked.

Rand brought the ship around into the wind and started down the shelf, constantly accelerating. The tail lifted from the ground. The motor was running wide open now. The tires held.

"Thank God," murmured Sandra, as the ship rose gracefully into the air. "Thank God for everything."